THE LIGHTSHIP

D0495277

'Our visitors come from Celle, two brothers, both armed and both said to be dangerous – nothing new to us there. One of them shot a postman. The mailbag hasn't been found yet.'

'I should like to know something about the other one,' said Freytag. 'Dr Caspary or whatever his name is.'

'Only two were mentioned, the brothers. They escaped at noon, in broad daylight, and from a pretty famous jail.'

'Dr Caspary and the other two don't fit together.' Rethorn sat up and began to button his jacket, then fished for his shoes and tied the laces and looked at Freytag expectantly.

'When shall we take them prisoner?' he asked.

*Also available
in Methuen Paperbacks
by Siegfried Lenz*

The German Lesson

SIEGFRIED LENZ

The Lightship

Translated by Michael Bullock

METHUEN

The Lightship

British Library Cataloguing in Publication Data

Lenz, Siegfried
  The lightship.
  I. Title   II. Das Feuerschiff. *English*
  833'.914[F]   PT2623.E583

  ISBN 0-413-59900-0
  ISBN 0-413-59910-8 Pbk

Original title *Das Feuerschiff*
Copyright © 1960 Hoffman and Campe Verlag, Hamburg
English translation copyright © 1962 Hoffman and Campe Verlag

This edition first published in Great Britain 1986
by Methuen London Ltd
11 New Fetter Lane, London EC4P 4EE

Printed in Great Britain by
Richard Clay (The Chaucer Press) Ltd,
Bungay, Suffolk

This book is available in both a hardback and paperback edition.
The paperback is sold subject to the condition
that it shall not, by way of trade or otherwise,
be lent, resold, hired out or otherwise circulated
without the publisher's prior consent in any form of
binding or cover other than that in which it is
published and without a similar condition
including this condition being imposed
on the subsequent purchaser.

They had been moored endlessly by the shifting sand-banks. For nine years, since the war, their ship had been moored by a long anchor chain, a blazing red hillock on the slate-grey plain of the sea, covered with barnacles, overgrown with seaweed – apart from short periods in dock she had been moored there all the time, during the hot summers, when the Baltic was smooth and dazzling and suppressed, and in all the winters, when heavy seas ran under the ship and ice floes scraped, splitting along her sides. She was an old reserve lightship which they had refitted and sent out again after the war to warn ships of the shifting sandbanks and to give them a steering point along the narrow channel between the mines.

For nine years the black ball had hung at her masthead, indicating that they were in position, the flashing light of her beacon had circled at night over the long bay and the dark surface of the sea as far as the islands that rose grey and flat as the blade of an oar on the horizon. Now the minefields had been cleared, the channel was considered safe, and in a fortnight the lightship was to be withdrawn. This was her last watch.

The last watch was to end before the onset of the winter storms that crashed into the bay with short, heavy seas, undermined the steep loamy coast, and left a crusty lightwater line of seaweed, splinters of ice, and arrow-shaped sea grass on the flat beach. Before the storms break, the Baltic out here beyond the long bay is calm;

5

the swell runs with a gentle gliding motion; the water turns blue-black in color. This is a good sign for fishing: the striped backs of the mackerel dart about in shoals just below the surface, the salmon rise to the spoon bait, and the cod are as firmly entangled in the meshes of the ground net as if they had been shot into them by a gun. Then it is high time for the coastal shipping, for the tubby sailing boats with auxiliary engines, the windjammers and timber schooners, to sail down from Finland with a final deck cargo of mine timber or cut planks and make for their winter havens. The channel outside the long bay and between the islands is full of them before the storms, and those on the lightship can see the pitching, rolling, struggling procession passing by on its way to the safe harbors beyond the horizon; and when they have disappeared the black-headed gulls fly in and the heavy saddlebacks, one at a time to begin with, then in screeching flocks, and they circle around the lightship, perch on its masts or settle on the water upon which the ship's red reflection lies.

When their last watch began, the sea was almost empty of the rolling tubs, only a few stragglers were still sailing by, clinging to the horizon, and the men on the lightship now saw almost nothing but the white railroad ferries that disappeared frothing and foaming behind the islands each morning and evening, and a few heavy freighters and broad-beamed fishing smacks that sailed indifferently past them.

On that hazy morning there was nothing in sight. The lightship was heaving lethargically on a long anchor chain, the current was piling up and thrusting against her hull, and a green, a sulfur-green glimmer lay over the sea. A flight of gray geese swooped along just above the water, past the ship and on to the islands, their wings making a whirring, whistling sound. The anchor chain rubbed to and fro, grated in the hawse-holes, when the gentle swell lifted the ship, producing a sound like a rusty nail being pried out of a crate with a crowbar. The continuous swell splashed against the stern. A wide track of foam ran out from the bay to the open sea like a white vein, with flapping bladder wrack, seaweed-covered pieces of wood, plants, bits of cork, and a bobbing bottle floating in it. It was the second morning of their last watch.

As Freytag opened the cabin door he glanced up at the lookout. The man on lookout did not lower his binoculars; slowly rotating, as though his feet were riveted to the deck, he turned the upper part of his body, turned it from the hips without moving his feet, and Freytag knew that nothing was wrong, and stepped out into the hazy morning. He was an old man with a scrawny neck and a taut-skinned face, tears flowed ceaselessly from his watery eyes as though in recollection of a desperate effort; although his stocky body was bent it still revealed some of the strength that had once been in it, or still was in it. His fingers were gnarled, his legs bowed, as though in his youth he had been made to ride on a barrel. Before he became skipper of the lightship he had been for sixteen years the master of a tramp steamer on the Levant run, and at this time he had got into the habit of walking around with a half-smoked, cold cigarette in his mouth, which he carefully put down beside his plate during meals.

He leaned his back against the cabin door, the cold cigarette moved to and fro from one corner of his mouth to the other, wagging as it went, and he looked across at the islands, over the trail of foam running out to sea, and then at the wreck-buoy beside which the spars of a ship sunk during the war towered up out of the water; and as he stood there he felt the door open behind him; he stepped to one side without turning around, because he knew that it was the boy he had been waiting for.

Freytag hadn't asked anyone's permission; as the skipper, he had simply brought Fred aboard for the last watch, taking him away from the hospital where the boy had been ill with mercury poisoning. Freytag had seen the pale, lanky boy with the harassed eyes lying in bed, and after talking with the doctor in the corridor he had come back and said to Fred, 'Tomorrow you're coming out on duty with me,' and although the boy had wanted neither to go back to the ramshackle factory where he worked as a thermometer-blower nor to Freytag's ship, he was now on board the ship at its station.

Fred let go of the cabin door, which shut with a hissing, sucking sound, and studied the old man with a harassed, hostile look out of the corners of his eyes. He didn't speak to him; he came and stood beside him and waited in an attitude of silent hostility. Never, so long as he could remember, had he stood beside his father in any other way, not when he had reached to his shoulder, and not now, when he could look down from above into his loose-fitting collar under which a strip of smooth, sunburned skin began that ran all over his back down to his waist.

Ever since he had learned what had happened down there in the Levant – at the time when his father ran the tramp line and he himself was still going to school – he had been finished with him, without their ever having talked about it or his ever having needed to talk about it.

They stood silently side by side, they knew one another too well for either to have expected anything of the other, and without speaking, with a brief nod of the head, Freytag asked the boy to follow him.

One behind the other they climbed up the yellow light tower, saw the distorted reflection of their faces in the hard, curved glass; they looked down over the sea and at the deck of the ship, whose heaving motion they felt more up here than down below, and Fred saw the heavy,

8

sagging chain dip into the water with a splash when the swell reached up to it. He also saw the man with the gleaming black rook standing at the bow and heard his father say: 'That's Gombert. He still hasn't given up. He means to teach the rook to talk by Christmas, and by Easter it's supposed to recite a psalm.' Fred didn't answer, he gazed indifferently at the man in the bow, who was talking eagerly to the rook as it hopped about on the deck with clipped, limply dangling wings. 'Her name is Edith,' said Freytag, 'Edith von Laboe.'

Then he climbed down, Fred behind him, and they walked silently to the wireless cabin, and found Philippi at the set, a small, slender man in a faded sweater, with headphones on, holding a pencil in one hand and rolling cigarettes on the table with the other.

'He's reporting the speed of the current,' said Freytag, 'the state of the sea and the weather.'

Philippi didn't turn around to them, although he could see their shadows on the wall and on the table littered with crumbs of tobacco; he took no notice of the loud-speaker, which was emitting a crackling noise, a dry clicking, as though big grasshoppers were walking over a tin roof; he sat there calmly in his windowless box of a cabin and after a while said, 'It's been aired out enough now,' and straightened his earphones.

'That's the wireless cabin,' said Freytag, 'now you've seen that too,' and he pushed the boy away from the entrance with his shoulder, closed the door which ran on rollers, looked around and wondered what Fred hadn't seen yet since coming aboard. He glanced around his ship, and for the first time it appeared to him old and doomed – a ship that wasn't free and able to run to other shores, but lay like a convict on a long chain, held by a huge anchor sunk deep in the sandy bottom, and Freytag could think of nothing else to show the boy. He shrugged his shoulders irresolutely. He looked across his ship like a man looking across flat land. He pulled out his handkerchief, wound it around his hand and put the bandaged hand back in his pockets; for a moment he listened for a sound from the boy, who had come to a stop behind him and a little to one side; he heard nothing, and he clenched the bandaged hand into a fist and felt the material stretch over the gnarled joints of his fingers. His eyes fell on the lookout, who had lowered the glass and was leaning against the slate, on which nothing had yet been written on this hazy morning, and he signed to Fred to follow him. Their footsteps clattered on the iron steps of the companion ladder; the steps were rusty, bent, and worn, the fluting that was supposed to give a grip to the soles had been worn away and was hardly visible. They mounted one behind the other, Freytag in front, and the lookout stood by the slate and watched their heads appear above the deck, watched their shoulders emerge and their bodies, till finally they pushed off from the handrail and landed beside him.

Fred hadn't seen Zumpe yet, he only knew that the man whom he met on lookout had been torpedoed on a ship carrying iron ore during the war and had afterwards drifted for ninety hours in the battered lifeboat and been thought dead by everyone. Freytag had told him this, and he had also told him that at the time Zumpe's wife had put an obituary notice in the paper which Zumpe himself, when he came home and read it, considered so mean that he left her. Now he regularly carried his own obituary about with him in a shabby wallet and passed it around with a grin: a yellowed piece of paper become limp and stained between many thumbs and forefingers.

Fred had heard about Zumpe for the first time on the trip out, when his father told him about the men he would meet on the ship, and now they were standing face to face shaking hands and Fred felt the man's horn-hard, claw-like fingers between his own. The too-short

10

limbs, the too-short neck and the heavy head made Zumpe look somehow dwarflike; his neck had deep folds in it and his face was lumpy.

'Give him the glasses,' said Freytag.

Zumpe drew the thin leather strap over his head and handed Fred the glasses, which he took without haste and turned around in his hands.

'Look through them,' said Freytag, 'the islands are over there.' The men exchanged a glance, and the boy raised the heavy binoculars to his eyes and saw in sharply focused lenses the beaches of the islands and the sand-colored causeway between them, and behind the causeway, salt-white and quietly gliding, he discerned a sail that seemed not to belong to a boat but to be moving along the causeway. Fred squeezed the glasses together on the steel swivel, so that the coin-round lenses impinged upon one another, till they overlapped, and then he looked out beyond the islands, turned at the waist, saw the wreck-buoy and spars of the sunken ship wander through the sharply defined circle and out of it as he swung the binoculars on towards the open sea. The trail of foam moved across the circle, a diving gull that struck the water with angled wings, and against the vast horizon he identified the sparkling crests of running waves. Then he came to a stop, suddenly interrupting the circling movement as if he had come up against an obstacle, and the men saw him lower the glasses, immediately raise them again and begin quickly to turn the notched center screw, and they came closer and looked in the direction in which Fred was gazing. They saw nothing.

'What is it?' asked Freytag.

'I can't see anything,' said Zumpe.

'A boat,' said Fred, 'a motorboat. I think it's drifting.'

He could clearly distinguish the gray boat that lay at an angle to the sea and was drifting away, lifted by the swell as it moved along; in the sharply focused lens he could also make out that the boat was occupied and that one of the crew was standing on the wooden engine cover with his legs apart waving something to and fro.

'Yes,' said Fred, 'it's a drifting boat and there are men on it.'

Zumpe took the glasses from his hand, his upper lip curled, baring his big incisors, as he put the binoculars to his eyes, looked through them for a few seconds and passed them without a word to Freytag; Freytag too only looked through them for a few seconds, then he handed the glasses back to the boy and said: 'We'll put out the boat.'

'The boat has been painted,' said Zumpe.

'Then we'll put out the painted boat,' said Freytag.

'The paint isn't quite dry yet.'

'You can warn them about that,' said Freytag, 'but first pick them up. Perhaps they won't really care what kind of a boat picks them up.'

'By myself?'

'Take Gombert with you, he can help you. As far as I'm concerned you can ask his rook too; maybe Edith would like to go with you.'

Zumpe walked over to the companion ladder; there was something laborious in his movements, something angular and jerky, and while he was climbing down Fred watched the boat, which was drifting diagonally out towards the open sea.

'They're drifting in the current,' said Freytag. 'There's a strong current running out from the bay, they're right in the middle of it.'

The boy said nothing, and Freytag went on: 'During the summer, when the sailing boats go by, you can sometimes see how strong it is: when there is only light air, and even when there's a gentle breeze, the current is stronger than the wind and carries the boat out.'

12

'They're signaling to us,' said Fred, who never stopped looking through the glasses.

'We shall pick them up,' said Freytag. 'It won't be the first time.'

'I ought to go too,' said Fred.

'You'd better stay here.'

Zumpe and Gombert now appeared down below by the davits, they levered the boat out of the cleats, swung it out and lowered it to the water with a winch. The boat was now attached only by the painter and scraped against the side of the lightship. While Gombert clambered down the accommodation ladder into the boat and took the tiller, Zumpe started the engine, cast off the painter, and squatted down on the floor boards so that only his head projected above the gunwhale; they chugged off, turned in a short arc, and headed for the drifting boat, leaving a swirling wake behind them.

Fred watched through the glasses as they rode the swell and then traveled along in the trail of foam, which their boat slit open for a second, and he saw the whitish streak close behind them and the boat grew flatter and shorter, till finally it was as flat as the deck plank with only Gombert's massive back rising above it. They held course for the drifting boat, and when they had reached it Fred saw them slowly circle around it, then make straight for it and draw alongside: three times he saw the outline of a figure rise and fall, and he said to Freytag: 'There are three of them; they're climbing aboard. I wonder what kind of people they are.'

'We shall soon know,' said Freytag. 'They'll thank you, because it was you who spotted them. Perhaps they were making for the island and ran into trouble.'

Fred quickly turned around to him, saw him standing there with the cold cigarette between his lips, his hands in his pockets.

'Would you like the glasses?' he asked.

'No,' said Freytag, 'you spotted them, now you must be on the job when they come in. Keep the glasses.'

The boy raised the binoculars to his eyes again; he noticed, as his father came a step nearer, that he looked at him for a long time from the side; he felt his longing to talk with him, heard him breathe in sharply and then say in a very low voice:

'This is very good for you, Fred, I ought to have done it before, I ought to have brought you out on a watch long ago, because you won't find air like this anywhere. There's nothing better for your lungs, Fred. You'll feel the difference when we get back.'

The boy said nothing. Out at sea the boats were drawing apart, and he thought they were going to abandon the drifting boat, but then it swung slowly around until it was in line astern, and Fred knew that they had made it fast and were bringing it in.

'I should have taken you out in the summer,' said Freytag. 'The air is much softer then, there's a lot of sun and visibility is good.'

Fred observed that the gray boat which they had in tow and were bringing in was bigger than their own, in which five men were now sitting; it looked like the lifeboat from a big passenger steamer, with thin handling guys and a sun-bleached fender at the bow.

'Are you listening to what I'm saying?' asked Freytag.

'Yes,' said Fred, 'I heard it all.' Now he could distinguish Gombert at the tiller, Zumpe in the bows, and the three men sitting between them. Without lowering the glasses or turning towards his father he asked: 'What shall we do with them?'

'We shall have to see,' said Freytag. 'We shall send them ashore as quickly as possible. We haven't a hotel on board. At the latest we shall hand them over to the bumboat. They can't stay here for the whole watch.'

The boats drew nearer, the taut tow rope was clearly

visible, even clearer were the faces, and now Rethorn appeared between the davits, and Soltow, the mechanic. Rethorn was wearing a well-ironed khaki jacket and a brown tie; he was the mate and they had never seen him on the lightship in any other state than starched and ironed. Finally, when the boats were in hailing distance, Trittel, their cook came out too – an emaciated man who kept his skinny hands folded under his flour-bespattered apron and looked as though he suffered from stomach trouble. They stood between the davits and waited for the arrival of the boats, which held course for the lightship's stern, turned in a short arc, and drew alongside. Ropes were dropped with a slapping sound, they made the boats fast, and then Freytag and the boy climbed down the companion ladder and also walked across to the davits, where the whole crew was gathered, apart from Philippi, who was still in his wireless cabin.

Fred leaned on the winch, he looked down at the ropes of the accommodation ladder, which were pulled taut and creaking like new leather under the weight of the first man to clamber on board from the boat below.

The first to come up was Dr Caspary. A chunky signet ring heralded his arrival, it encircled the middle finger of the hairy hand that first appeared over the gunwale, took a firm grip on the rope, pulled and went white on the knuckles with the effort, till the other hand grasped the rope after it and his face rose into view, a smiling face under bushy eyebrows, unshaven and partly hidden by a pair of water-splashed sunglasses. Rethorn helped him aboard and Dr Caspary looked around with a smile, went to each of the crew and introduced himself, still smiling. Then he went back to the rope ladder and together with Rethorn helped the others aboard: a giant with a bluish harelip, a shirt with no collar and an expression of stupid tenderness, and after him they helped up a long-haired young man who winced with disgust when Rethorn

15

touched him, stepped aside and smoothed the sleeve of his jacket.

They didn't introduce themselves, but Dr Caspary seemed to enjoy introductions; he jerked one thumb at the giant, said, 'Herr Kuhl, Eugen Kuhl,' whereupon Eugen nodded vigorously, after which Dr Caspary jerked the other thumb in the direction of the long-haired lad and said, 'Edgar Kuhl. The gentlemen are brothers.' Edgar eyed Dr Caspary with a look full of contemptuous repudiation; he shook hands with no one, looked no one in the face, but when Freytag invited them to follow him into the mess Edgar whipped his head around in a flash, as though to make sure there was no one behind him.

Freytag led them into the mess, a wood-paneled room whose walls were covered with pennants and the darkened portraits of long-forgotten skippers; he silently took out glasses from a wall cupboard, and a half bottle of cognac, put them on the table, and gestured invitingly towards the screwed-down armchairs. The giant with the harelip raised the empty glass to his eye with the stem towards Freytag; he stared through it with an intense effort, sighed, then a gentle idiotic grin appeared on his face: 'A chicken,' he said, 'you look exactly like a big chicken,' and he pushed the glass towards him, and Freytag filled it. All but Edgar sat down around the table. Edgar remained standing by the door, leaning against the wall with one leg crossed over the other in an attitude of nonchalant alertness. He had an open flick knife in his hand and began to pare his nails with it, watching the men at the table as he did so.

'What's the matter?' said Freytag. 'Won't you have a glass too?'

'He never drinks,' said Dr Caspary. 'All the time I've known him he has never touched a drop – and won't let himself be touched either. I guess Eddie has sworn an oath. But we're under no such obligation, and with this little drink I should like to thank you for bringing us high and dry.'

'He's the one who spotted you,' said Freytag, 'the lad.'

'Your son?' asked Dr Caspary.

'Yes, he was the first to see you.'

'I shall never forget it,' said Dr Caspary. He clinked glasses with Fred, Freytag, and Rethorn, nodded encouragingly to the giant, and they all drank.

The clicking sound of the winch echoed from the davits outside as they hauled in the boat to the accompaniment of talk and shouted instructions; Eddie walked suspiciously from the door to a porthole, looked out for a moment, and returned to his place.

'It was no great feat,' said Freytag. 'A thing like that can happen around here any time; there's a strong current out there.'

'We had been drifting since dawn,' said Dr Caspary. 'Thank God the sea was calm, eh, Eddie?'

Again he received a brief glance full of contemptuous rejection, which, however, he did not seem to notice; he was still wearing the sunglasses, which were now sprinkled with small, dull patches – the last traces of the salt water – and on his face he still wore the smile that he had carried in front of him as he climbed aboard.

'No,' said Freytag, 'it was no great feat. Nothing more than a practice accident.'

'Very good,' said Dr Caspary. 'That's what it was, a trial shipwreck. I hope you didn't also pick us up on trial.'

'We'll hail a boat,' said Freytag. 'It can take you to a port, to Kiel or Flensburg, or across to the islands. In any case, there's always the bumboat.'

'It comes in four days,' said Rethorn.

'Four days, then,' said Freytag, ' – if nothing else comes along in the meantime.'

He refilled the glasses, as though he had got used to

the idea that the men would have to stay on board for four days, and as though he now wanted to drink to this accomplished fact; but Dr Caspary said: 'We shouldn't like to inflict that on you. We don't want to stay here four days and there's no need to hail a boat for us. As far as I remember we have a boat of our own. It's simply that the cooling system has broken down. If that can be repaired here we shall leave you.'

'If we hail a boat,' said Freytag, 'a fishing smack say, which can take you ashore, you would already be on land by tomorrow.'

'We're not interested in that,' said Dr Caspary. 'Or are you interested in that, Eddie?'

Eddie made a negative movement with the flick knife.

'What about you, Eugen?'

The giant looked at Dr Caspary tenderly and shook his head, and in a tone that sounded as if his split mouth was cutting each word in two he said: 'Not interested.'

'That settles it,' said Dr Caspary, 'you won't hail a boat; it will be quite enough if you will help us to repair our boat.'

'Are you going far?' asked Freytag.

'To Faaborg,' said Dr Caspary, 'through the channel between the islands. We're expected there.'

He turned his hand with the chunky signet ring around on the table, looked at it with his head on one side, and after a while began to breathe on the ring and polish it on his hip, scrutinizing it from time to time with his hand stretched out flat on the table. The giant with the hairlip watched all this full of affectionate interest, and Freytag, Rethorn, and Fred also watched Dr Caspary polishing the signet ring, which sat like a gleaming tumor on his hairy hand.

Outside, a sound like a mallet striking wood rang out, the boat settled with a jolt in the cleats, the winch swung
18

back loose, and the ropes with the turnbuckles attached clattered as they were drawn across the deck.

'Will you be able to help us?' asked Dr Caspary.

'Our mechanic is already in your boat,' said Rethorn.

'Soltow?' asked Freytag.

'I sent him down,' said the mate. 'Zumpe is helping him.'

'Give me another drink, you,' the giant said to Freytag. 'Just a little one, no more than goes in your little glasses.'

Dr Caspary surreptitiously gave a negative sign to Freytag and said: 'I shouldn't drink any more, Eugen. It isn't very good stuff, and we ought not to drink anything that isn't very good. It makes our teeth loose, Eugen.'

The giant looked at him dumbfounded, then cast an indignant glance at Freytag and covered the glass with his heavy hand.

'Yes,' said Dr Caspary, 'that's right, Eugen, that's sensible.'

Eugen pushed the glass away and drew his sleeve across his sweaty forehead; he stood up, took off his short, crumpled jacket, hung it over the back of his chair, and sat down again.

'Yes,' said Dr Caspary gently, 'yes, Eugen.'

He raised his head, because Eddie suddenly stepped away from the door and stood crouching under the porthole as though expecting danger, and his eyes and his knife were directed towards the varnished door, which now opened a crack, slowly, oscillating, as if it had been pushed not by a hand but by the wind, till all of a sudden Zumpe's lumpy face appeared and turned from the crack towards the table at which the men were sitting.

Freytag rose reluctantly.

'Anything wrong?' asked Dr Caspary.

'The captain is wanted in the wireless cabin,' said Zumpe.

'I thought as much,' said Freytag. He heaved himself

up and was going to the door when a hand drew him back by the sleeve. Dr Caspary held him fast with a smile and said: 'Just so as you don't forget, we're really not interested in your hailing a boat for us. You have heard our decision. When our boat has been repaired we shall immediately continue our voyage.'

'I understand,' said Freytag.

'Very good,' said Dr Caspary. 'It isn't often that people understand one another so quickly.'

Zumpe waited outside until Freytag was beside him and had shut the door of the mess. Without a word, he walked ahead of him to the wireless cabin; the wireless cabin was empty, the instruments switched off.

'Where is Philippi?' asked Freytag.

Zumpe nodded his head in the direction of the accommodation ladder, where they had made fast the men's boat and were repairing it, and from where the sound of muffled conversation reached them. He listened for a moment, drew Freytag into the wireless cabin and turned the key. They stood motionless in the darkness, stood close together and heard nothing but their own breathing, then the switch clicked and the electric light flared up. Zumpe bent down, opened a cupboard, pulled out a bundle, listened again and picked the bundle up and put it on the table, a longish bundle wrapped in canvas and tied tightly with leather thongs. Still without a word, Zumpe began to untie the thongs; he opened up the canvas, came upon dully gleaming paper soaked in oil, opened this up too – quickly with practiced movements, as though he had done it before – and then his hand plunged groping and rustling under another layer of paper, lay still, began slowly and jerkily to pull, and drew out a submachine gun, which it held by the barrel. The barrel shimmered bluish in the electric light.

Zumpe laid the gun on the table, his hand groped its way under the oil-soaked paper again.

'That's not all,' he said, 'now come the best things, for connoisseurs,' and he pulled out a shotgun with a sawed-off barrel and laid it likewise on the table. The shotgun had a carved stock that was inlaid with silver, and Zumpe stroked the stock with his short fingers and said: 'How cool it is, how good to touch.'

'Where did you get that stuff?' asked Freytag.

'I found it in their boats,' said Zumpe. 'It was hidden under the floor boards, and I was standing on them all the way back to the ship.'

'Put it back,' said Freytag.

'Everything?'

'Put it back. It's none of our business what they have in their boat.'

'We ought not let them leave,' said Zumpe.

'We'll get rid of them as fast as we can,' said Freytag. 'It's none of our business where they came from or where they are going to.'

'They're armed,' said Zumpe, 'I saw that while they were changing boats.'

'I know,' said Freytag. 'I saw it too.'

'We ought to keep them here till the bumboat comes, and when they're off the ship Philippi should talk to the harbor police.'

'I want peace on our last watch,' said Freytag.

'We can hail a boat,' said Zumpe.

'They're not interested in that.'

'There are seven of us and three of them.'

'You've forgotten to count their pistols.'

'And what about this?' said Zumpe, lovingly stroking the stock of the sawed-off shotgun.

'That makes no difference,' said Freytag, 'they have the cartridges in their pockets; now put the stuff back – all of it.'

Zumpe stood hesitating, looking in perplexity at Freytag, who made the cold cigarette wag between his lips, then he turned around and began to pack everything up again and tie it with the leather thongs.

'What's the matter with their boat?' asked Freytag. 'Can you repair the cooling system?'

'It's not the cooling system,' replied Zumpe. 'The shaft is all to blazes. Soltow took it out and now he is putting it back in again, because there's nothing to be done with it.'

'Nothing?'

'Nothing,' said Zumpe.

'Why didn't you tell me that right away?'

'You didn't ask me.'

'That changes everything,' said Freytag. 'Now put that stuff back in the boat and tell Soltow to go on working, or at least to pretend he is still working.'

'What's going to happen now?' asked Zumpe.

'Dinner.'

A fishing smack ran close by the lightship, gray and white and with a swishing bow wave; the hard knocking sound of the engine echoed over the sea, and the mast traveled past the portholes of the mess like a white clock hand. The giant with the harelip was the only one still eating, the only one who took no notice of the passing smack: eagerly he piled the glassy noodles on his plate, picked the crisp pieces of fried bacon out of the deep aluminum bowl; he snapped up the dangling noodles from below, twisting his head and raising his face towards the ceiling, and he was very happy while he ate.

Freytag, Rethorn, and the boy watched the fishing smack's mast travel stiffly past. Dr Caspary merely looked up once, then glanced at Eugen with a smile and polished the chunky signet ring lightly on his hip.

Since Eddie had left the mess not another word had been uttered; they sat there as though waiting for news and felt the ship rising and falling slightly in the swell. Eddie had gone out even before they began the meal and they could see him standing by the accommodation ladder, leaning nonchalantly against the shrouds and working on his fingernails with the knife.

The sky had grown lighter, a dirty reddish trail ran across it, and the water outside was wrinkled by gusts from the rising wind. The islands now stood out flat and clear, the reflection of the lightship on the sea acquired

23

sharper outlines, long waves struck the stern and splashed up before subsiding. The wreck-buoy by the spars of the sunken ship heeled over in the current, bobbing and swaying, while the thrusting water dragged at the moorings.

The giant swallowed and sighed and pushed his empty plate across to Freytag, his face twisted, he wiped his split mouth with the back of his hand.

'Well?' asked Dr Caspary gently.

'It could have been better,' said Eugen. 'The fat was cold and the noodles tasted like fishworms.'

'It's a favorite dish at sea,' said Dr Caspary.

'It's eatable here,' said Eugen.

The chugging of the fishing smack outside stopped, and Dr Caspary looked suspiciously at Freytag, abruptly rose, went to a porthole without taking his eyes off the skipper, but before he looked out at the smack the chugging started up again. Dr Caspary smiled and returned to his chair.

'I thought you had invited visitors,' he said, and as Freytag made no reply, he added: 'We don't mind. Or do you mind, Eugen?'

'No,' said the giant, 'I don't mind,' and went on for a long time shaking his head and staring attentively at the cold, glassy noodles in the aluminum bowl as if counting them.

'Your predecessors?' asked Dr Caspary pointing at the darkened photographs of the skippers with which one wall of the mess was covered.

'Yes,' said Freytag, 'those are my predecessors.'

'They look sad, very sad. They all have mournful eyes, and their lips – there's a touch of bitterness about their lips. Have you noticed? What is that due to?'

'They had too few visitors,' said Freytag, 'or not enough to drink.'

'You are the first one who looks different.'

'I can't complain in that respect.'

'Very good,' said Dr Caspary. 'I have the greatest esteem for people who are content, even if I don't know what to make of it.'

'He ate very few noodles,' said Eugen, looking at Freytag reproachfully. 'Far too few.'

'I noticed right away how sadly your predecessors look down from the wall,' said Dr Caspary. 'They all look discontented. Perhaps it's the fault of this ship?'

'The ship is old but trustworthy,' said Freytag. 'She has more storms behind her than any other ship I know.'

'But she is permanently moored,' said Dr Caspary. 'She is chained to the bottom and can't break free and lies here winter and summer, while the others sail by. A ship ought to be sailing to and fro between harbors, she ought to go away and come back, she ought to have stories to tell. A ship is for sailing to foreign parts. This ship was built for the chain from the beginning, she was laid down with the aim of having a trustworthy prisoner to whom every port is closed.'

'Like a man sentenced for life,' said the giant.

'The others travel around, and you are on a chain,' said Dr Caspary. 'Perhaps that is why your predecessors have such sad faces: because of this imprisonment under the same horizon, under the same shore.'

'Prisoners have a power of their own,' said Freytag. 'The masters are far more dependent upon their prisoners than the prisoners on the masters. If we didn't exist you would have a well-filled ships' cemetery here, and the spars of sunken ships would stick out all over the bay like nails from a fakir's bed. The whole bay would be full of wrecks, and out there, where the minefields used to be, they would lie side by side or even one on top of another. The others can only sail about because we lie at anchor and they can rely on our signals. Where a lightship

25

lies, there is something wrong. They know that, and they are on the alert as soon as they see us.'

'But the others are free,' said Dr Caspary.

'The others are dependent upon us,' said Freytag. 'We hold them in the palm of our hand, and if we want to we can send them onto sandbanks or into the minefield or into a channel where they will be reduced to scrap value overnight. That's all there is to it,' said Freytag.

Fred and Rethorn exchanged a glance, they were both rising at the same time when the giant stretched out his index finger in their direction, looked at them reproachfully and said: 'And what about you two? Why are you so quiet? You haven't said anything yet and now you want to leave.'

A cry echoed across the deck, then a slapping noise as if a wet net were being vigorously beaten out, and Freytag and Dr Caspary jumped to their feet like a flash, while Eugen instinctively whipped around in his chair and ducked, and then the door flew open, crashed against the wall of the mess, and before it bounced back Zumpe staggered in with his hands stretched out in front of him and fell over the table. The firmly screwed-down table caught him and bent his body at the waist, his lumpy forehead struck the wooden tabletop. Zumpe's arms lay outstretched beside his head, so that he stood or crouched there in the position of a man about to dive into the water; and before Rethorn had time to reach him, or he himself had time to raise his head, Eddie appeared in the doorway, both hands on the back of his neck, his greasy hair over his forehead and breathing sharply through his teeth, as though fighting against pain. Rethorn waited till he was in the mess, he saw now that Eddie was not carrying a knife, and walked slowly towards him, his head drawn into his shoulders. He slowly crouched. Eddie didn't take his hands from his neck.

'Look out,' warned Freytag, and Rethorn turned

around and looked into the sweaty, glistening face of Eugen, into the small yellow eyes, which at that moment reminded him of a goat's eyes, and he saw the dry spittle at the corners of the giant's mouth. Eugen had the fingers of one hand outspread; in the other he held an automatic pistol. His mouth was open and his bared teeth shimmered white.

'Come along,' he said to Rethorn, 'I like you so much. We got on so well during the meal. Sit down again. Come on, quick, go back to your seat and leave Eddie alone, my little brother. Will you do that?'

'Please,' said Dr Caspary politely, 'please sit down. We can negotiate more comfortably sitting down.'

Eddie had gone up close to Zumpe, who was lying motionless with his face on the table, and without taking his hands from his neck he looked down at him and said: 'He touched me. He struck me,' and he kicked the back of Zumpe's knee, so that the motionless man's knee struck the corner of the table leg, causing the upper part of his body to rise and collapse on the tabletop again, as though through a prolonged reflex.

'Stop it,' said Freytag, and again to Dr Caspary: 'Tell him to stop it.'

'Stop it, Eddie,' said Dr Caspary gently.

'He touched me,' said Eddie. 'He tried to knock me down with a rope.'

'Has something happened?' asked Dr Caspary.

'He was working on the boat with the others,' said Eddie. 'I was standing up above watching them as they fumbled around – the most brilliant engineers seafaring has ever seen.'

'Is the boat ready?' asked Dr Caspary.

'It will never be ready,' said Eddie. 'Seafaring made a great catch when it got hold of those two; if all mechanics were like them we should have a magnificent navy on land. They only worked with hammers.'

'What about the boat?' asked Dr Caspary impatiently.

'We can write it off. I watched how they fiddled around and kept putting their heads together, until this one here' – he nodded down at Zumpe – 'pulled something loose and dropped it overboard. I think it was the spark plugs. I called him up, and if I hadn't been careful I shouldn't be here now. He hit out with a rope, he touched me.' And he lashed out with his foot again and kicked Zumpe on the shin.

'Leave him alone, Eddie,' said Dr Caspary. 'Sit down, and you sit down too, Eugen.'

The giant sat down and pushed the automatic into the back pocket of his trousers; Eddie went back to the door, leaned against it, and stood there with one leg crossed over the other.

'I must go,' said Rethorn. 'I have work to do.'

'You can go,' said Freytag.

Rethorn waited until Dr Caspary looked at him and confirmed: 'You can go, but remind your wireless operator that we're not interested in his hailing a boat.'

Then Rethorn left the mess and Fred with him, and Freytag bent down over Zumpe, raised him from the table and pressed the limp body into one of the screwed-down armchairs. Freytag patted his face and jerked at his shoulders, till Zumpe shook himself and sat up, but without raising his eyes or speaking.

'Here I am,' cried Eddie. 'We're still on board.'

'Leave him alone now,' said Dr Caspary. 'We must see about the boat.'

'He knows best what is the matter with the boat,' said Eddie from the door.

'Have you tried to start the engine?'

'We couldn't even get as far as the islands with that boat.'

'That's a pity,' said Dr Caspary. 'In a certain sense

even unpleasant – I mean for you, Captain. You were going to help us with the repairs.'

Freytag said nothing.

'And you see what's come of it,' Dr Caspary went on. 'One of your men was obviously not in agreement with your intention. He has prevented us from being able to sail on in our own boat. That was a mistake, because now we shall be forced to borrow your boat. We're expected in Faaborg and I can see no other way of being there in time except with your boat. We'll lower it again.'

Freytag looked quickly at the davits, in which their boat hung firmly lashed, and he recognized Soltow's back bending over the engine, and for a second he caught sight of Soltow's hand on the gunwale and in the hand a heavy screwdriver. When he turned his head back he noticed that Dr Caspary was also looking at the davits, and for the first time he felt free from those eyes that seemed to reach him everywhere and all the time through the patchy sunglasses.

'Ah,' said Dr Caspary, 'now I suppose your boat is also out of order.'

'It's an old dinghy,' said Freytag.

'I know; that's why it understands what we are saying.'

'You can't take our boat,' said Freytag. 'We should be lost without it.'

'I'm very sorry, but we should also be lost without it. We're expected.'

'Not our boat.'

'We only want to borrow it,' said Dr Caspary.

'The boat will not be lowered.'

Dr Caspary smiled, polished the signet ring thoughtfully on his hip, then he straightened up and said to the Kuhls: 'Go out and inspect the boat, and if it is in working order, launch it.' He pointed to Zumpe. 'Take him with you, he'll be the first to help you. I want to talk to the Captain alone for a moment.'

The brothers went up to Zumpe, one on each side; they took him under the armpits, lifted him and left the mess, Zumpe's feet barely touching the floor.

'They won't lower the boat,' said Freytag when they were alone. 'They know what it would mean to us to be without a boat.'

'It means exactly the same to you as it does to us,' said Dr Caspary. 'And therefore I shall make you a proposal, Captain. See that we get away from here and you shall be left in peace. Don't try to put us in chains like your ship, and above all: warn your men. If the crew sabotage your orders something might happen that would not be in your interest. I have my reasons for warning you, because I alone know Eugen and his brother. See to it that we get away from here before we grow impatient.'

'And what will happen if you grow impatient?' asked Freytag. Dr Caspary drew out a long cigarette holder and a case; he conscientiously screwed a cigarette into the opening of the holder, lit it, and said, after fleetingly inhaling several times: 'Do you want me to go into details?'

'Shall I tell you where you have come from?' asked Freytag.

'I know that,' replied Dr Caspary.

'You don't want to hear the truth.'

'The whole truth is without charm,' said Dr Caspary. 'All my life it has been an ambition of mine never to learn or speak more than half the truth. If I hadn't done that I should have died of boredom.'

'You have something on your conscience and you want to disappear.'

'You see?' said Dr Caspary. 'I knew you were incapable of speaking anything but the plain truth. Another reason for us to get away from here.'

They both turned simultaneously towards an open porthole outside which a shadow suddenly rose, soundless
30

and menacing, a shadow that fell right across the mess-room table, for a second lay between them like a frontier, and vanished before they had discovered whose it was. Not a footstep, not a word, was to be heard, only the sounds of the water outside as it was thrown gurgling against the ship.

'Talk to your men,' said Dr Caspary. 'It's advisable and we shall save ourselves surprises which we can do without. You can see for yourself that it's necessary.'

Eddie came into the mess and stood by the door. He had the flick knife in his hand, made a movement from the wrist meaning 'no' and said: 'There's nothing doing with their boat. We don't need to lower it.'

'I suppose it also has engine trouble,' said Dr Caspary.

'In sympathy with ours,' said Eddie.

'Then we shall do without the boats and utilize the last resort.'

'What do you mean by the last resort?' asked Freytag.

'Your ship,' said Dr Caspary. 'You will weigh anchor, and you will take us across in the lightship and set us ashore. If you feel self-conscious we can sail by night. Perhaps your ship will be grateful to you: for the first time it will sail free towards the horizon like the others and have strange water under its keel at last.'

'Do you know what that means?' said Freytag after a while. He took the cold cigarette out of his mouth, crushed it between his fingers and threw it down on the floor.

'A comfortable crossing,' said Dr Caspary, 'anyhow, more comfortable than in an open boat.'

'Do you know what it means when a lightship leaves its place?' reiterated Freytag. 'Can you imagine it?'

'I have had a good deal to complain of, but never lack of imagination,' said Dr Caspary. 'I can imagine that your colleagues sailing here from far away will be surprised if you are no longer on the spot. Perhaps they will also be

31

perplexed if you don't light them home. At the worst, they can drop anchor and wait till you get back.'

'If a lightship leaves it position, that's the end of safety for the others.'

'There are people who have a longing for danger.'

'This ship mustn't leave its position without the Coast Guard Office knowing.'

'The Coast Guard Office need not know.'

'Ships come in,' said Freytag. 'They steer by us.'

'Then for the time being they will have to find their way by themselves.'

'Do you know what that means in this channel?'

'My imagination is adequate for that.'

'You will never compel us to leave our position, not one of us.'

'Are you so sure beforehand?' said Dr Caspary.

'He's a smart boy,' said Eddie from the door.

'And you won't dare to do it either,' said Freytag. 'Do you know what will happen when the people on the first ship discover that we're not in position?'

'That question will be meaningless in Faaborg.'

'They would report it at once and search ships would put out and airplanes would go up, and they would have us before you were off the ship.'

'We haven't tried it yet.'

'Then try it,' said Freytag. 'Raise the anchor and hoist the auxiliary sail and set off. You'll never force us to do it.'

'Is the ship suffering from engine trouble too, by any chance?' asked Dr Caspary.

'The ship has no engine,' said Freytag. 'It isn't built for traveling, but for the anchor chain.'

'A born prisoner,' said Dr Caspary.

'I warn you,' said Freytag, 'if this ship leaves its position – '

'What then?'

32

'Then there will be consequences that no one can foresee. If a ship goes down in the open sea it is an isolated disaster and part of the price which seamen have to pay, but if a lightship vanishes from its station, order at sea comes to an end.'

'Order, Captain, is the triumph of the unimaginative; we hold different opinions on this point too. And now I shall make you another proposal. Go to your men and talk to them. We are ready to sail in our own boat and to regard your ship as the last resort. But if we are not to be reduced to the last resort our ship must be repaired. So talk to your mechanic and tell him that we are expected and that, since we do not wish to be excessively impolite, the matter is urgent. I don't want to give you a time limit, but you may assume that we have set ourselves a time limit. With your permission we shall live in this mess; it is amazing what can come to seem cozy under the pressure of circumstances.'

Dr Caspary smiled, and Freytag left the messroom without replying, walked past Eddie without a glance as he nonchalantly made way for him, stepped out into the midships. A cloud of smoke hung on the horizon, loose and pressed down onto the water by the wind; Gombert was on lookout; on the beach of the island black dots were seething around a broad black mass that looked like a boat; the hum of an airplane was in the air, and over the water, which was iron-gray towards the open sea and bluish black towards the shore, slow shadows were passing. Trittel was sitting by the rail with a hand line; he wore a jacket over his white things, and the piece of wood from which the line with the flashing tin fish at the end led down into the water rose and fell jerkily in his hand and jumped sideways. Under his folding stool shimmered the speckled bodies of cod he had already caught. On the davits Freytag discovered the giant with the harelip. He was standing with his legs apart pissing over the side and now carried the sawed-off shotgun, which rested loosely on his hip. Freytag avoided him and went to Rethorn's cabin.

When he entered the cabin he saw Rethorn lying in the bunk with his jacket unbuttoned and Fred sitting on a stool in front of him.

Freytag could feel that they had been talking together and were unwilling to continue now that he was standing before them; he calmly took his cap from his head and sat down on the edge of the bunk. He pulled a cigarette from Rethorn's packet and lit it and sat motionless between the man and the boy.

'Fine visitors we've invited,' said Rethorn after a while.

'We shall invite them to leave again,' said Freytag.

'The most outstanding visitors since I've been on board.'

'Have you heard something?'

'The gentlemen have even been mentioned on the radio, or at least two of them. Oddly enough, not only are the descriptions accurate but even their names.'

'When did you hear this?'

'It was announced at the end of the news. Our visitors come from Celle, two brothers, both armed and both said to be dangerous – nothing new to us there. One of them shot a postman. The mailbag hasn't been found yet.'

'I should like to know something about the other one,' said Freytag. 'Dr Caspary or whatever his name is.'

'Only two were mentioned, the brothers. They escaped at noon, in broad daylight, and from a pretty famous jail.'

'Dr Caspary and the other two don't fit together,' Rethorn sat up and began to button his jacket, then fished for his shoes and tied the laces and looked at Freytag expectantly.

'When shall we take them prisoner?' he asked.

34

Freytag looked up in surprise with an anguished smile; he stared past Rethorn, his fixed and absent eyes rested on the white-painted wall of the cabin, his taut-skinned face was motionless as if he were seeing something that made him forget everything else – the man, the boy, and the question – and he remained like this sitting between them, till Rethorn bounded out of the bunk, tapped him on the arm and said: 'Well, when?'

'When indeed,' said Freytag.

'As far as I'm concerned it can be right away.'

'What do you mean to do?' asked Freytag wearily.

'We'll take them one after the other.'

'One at a time,' said the boy, 'when they're not expecting it.'

'A pistol is always expecting something,' said Freytag. Now Fred stood up, listened for a moment at the door, squatted in the middle of the cabin at his father's feet, and whispered: 'You can't let them get away, you know who they are and now it's too late. If we want to, we can prevent them from leaving the ship. We'll take them prisoner and send them ashore with the bumboat.'

'Yes,' said Freytag, 'yes, what could be simpler?'

'What do you mean?' asked Fred.

'Don't you want to?' asked Rethorn.

'I don't know,' said Freytag. 'It's not so easy to talk to the muzzle of a gun. You can't argue with it.'

'What do you want to do then?' asked Fred gruffly and jumped up and went and stood beside Rethorn, who was washing his hands in a bucket.

'I want to have peace on the last watch,' said Freytag. 'Yes, peace. And I want all of us to get back to shore safe and sound when the ship is towed in. I don't want anyone to be missing when we land.'

'Did you see what they did to Zumpe?' asked Rethorn as he dried his hands and pulled his fingers so that the joints cracked.

'I was there,' said Freytag. 'Zumpe made a mistake.'

'Yes,' said Rethorn contemptuously, 'he did make a mistake, and that was to go out and bring in their boat. He should have let it drift.'

'I would bring it in again,' said Freytag. 'I wouldn't leave anyone adrift, even if I knew who he was.'

'One of them is a murderer,' said Fred. 'Are you going to let him get away? Perhaps you'd like to give him a hotwater bottle to take with him in the boat.'

'Stop talking like that,' said Freytag in a low voice. 'You don't belong to the ship.'

'The boy is right,' said Rethorn. 'We mustn't let them leave the ship. We must stop them from getting across to the other side. We can do it.'

'Suppose their pistols think differently?' said Freytag, staring at the white-painted wall again.

Rethorn tightened his tie, smoothed the hair on his temples with the balls of his thumbs, and said: 'We'll do something, it's our duty.'

Freytag shrugged his shoulders wearily. 'Stop it,' he said, 'that word makes me want to vomit. I can't hear it any more without retching.'

'Well, then,' said Rethorn, 'what do you suggest? What doesn't make you feel sick?'

'Soltow will repair their boat. He can do it in the ship's workshop.'

'Do you mean that seriously?'

Fred looked at the old man in surprise, an expression of the old hostility, the old contempt, appeared on his pale face; he turned quickly to the door and put his hand on the latch, but he stayed.

'So you want to let them stay on board,' said Rethorn as he began to clean the cuffs of his trousers with a pocket brush.

'I want to bring the whole crew ashore,' said Freytag, 'that's all.'

36

'You know what it means,' said Rethorn. 'It's your responsibility.'

'I don't want any of us to be missing when we land. And therefore you will speak to Soltow. He is to repair their boat. He is to be quick about it. That's all.'

It grew dark in the cabin. Rain was pattering on the porthole, and a dim, flickering light as of a myriad tiny explosions lay over the sea.

During the night, as he lay with a cold cigarette in his mouth, his arms crossed under his head, and looked across at the bunk in which the boy lay silent like himself – during the night he listened once again to the creaking of the hooked-back door.

Ever since the time of the tramp line Freytag had only been able to sleep with the door open; he opened it himself and hooked it back, but the hook hung loosely in the eye and creaked and jerked as the ship moved in the swell. That night he also heard the wind in the shrouds and the clinking of the chain in the chain locker. After the rain the sea had been smooth and lustreless, until a gusty wind had blown up off the land that quickly whipped up the water and brought choppy waves slapping against the ship. Freytag had waited till the big railway ferry had disappeared behind the islands, then he had gone down below, had taken off only his trousers and jacket and lain down on the bunk in his underclothes; he lay there uncovered, listening to the grating, creaking, and dragging sounds in the ship's timbers and looking across at Fred, who had curled up in a ball and turned to the wall. Ever since they had left Rethorn's cabin – Freytag alone, the boy long after him with the mate – they hadn't spoken another word to each other, and although Freytag noticed that the boy was awake he made no attempt to speak to him, nor did he expect Fred to say anything to him. He could still feel the

38

repudiation, the disappointment, in the silence that now existed; even in the stillness of the cabin the old enmity could be felt, and Freytag thought of the market at Djibouti, where two people who have something to settle retire behind a black cloth and continue in silence what they began with speech.

He knew he wouldn't be able to sleep; he lay and waited till he heard the footsteps of Zumpe, who was relieving Gombert on lookout, then he got up and dressed. Gombert's footsteps moved away – booming footsteps on the scrubbed deck which he always heard when the lookout was relieved; and he imagined he could now see the two men standing and whispering – on the alert, pressed against a wing of the bridge and ceaselessly watching the mess, whose portholes where darkened. Cautiously, as though to avoid disturbing the boy, he left the cabin and went out on deck and stood in the shadow of the door. The sky was overcast, the air damp and cool. The sharp flashing beam of their signal light ran out towards the open sea, falling from the light tower onto the dark water like a knife blade, narrow and distinct close to the vessel, broad and increasingly faint towards the horizon, and finally ending like a footprint in the sand expunged by the wind. The water flashed and flickered in the harsh light, a stabbing reflection emanated from it as from used oil in the sunshine, and the spray thrown up by the colliding waves dissolved in a shower of sparks. The light cut a path through the darkness over the water; sea birds swooped into it, rose in fright, sank down onto the water again exhausted in the darkness, and left foaming tracks behind them as they landed. Freytag looked forward at the high bows and the short-ened bowsprit, which on his first visit to the ship had reminded him of the half cut-off sword of a swordfish and now reminded him of this again: the shortened bowsprit gave the ship tubby lines, made it look like a sailing vessel that had run into something head on and been compressed by the impact. On the islands opposite, the headlights of a car blazed out, swung across, and went out at the same moment as the flashing beam of the ship ended and the light tower towered up again dark and stumpy.

Freytag thrust himself away from the wall with his shoulder and stepped out of the shadow; from the port side, where the galley lay, he heard groping footsteps, a curse and an agreed signal called out in a low voice, and he walked across and stood outside the bulkhead of the galley. He had no doubt that they were sitting inside, but he didn't go in; he remained standing by the bulkhead, wound his handkerchief around the gnarled joints of his fingers and thrust his hand into his pocket. He made no attempt to listen at the bulkhead, but even if he had made the attempt nothing would have reached him, because their understanding – and he knew that they were now coming to an understanding – was reached as soundlessly as if they were communicating solely by signs. After a while he left his position and stationed himself under the shrouds, from where he could keep an eye on the galley bulkhead, and when the flashing beam flared up he ducked under the rail. Water was splashing up over the bows, striking his face with a cold, fine spray; he felt the moisture on his neck and on his lips, but he stayed down below under the shrouds until the bulkhead sprang open and the first man came out.

The first man was Philippi. Behind him came Rethorn and Soltow, and Freytag saw them press themselves close up against the wall and stand there in a file of motionless menace. A sign – he couldn't make out who gave the sign with some curved object – and they set off one behind the other towards the mess. Freytag followed them. He walked upright in the harsh light cast over the deck from the light tower, walked behind them without

40

calling out, without warning, until Soltow heard his footsteps, turned around in a crouching position and recognized him, and at the second of recognition uttered a low whistle. Soltow came to a stop, pushed a square-head wrench up his sleeve; Rethorn and Philippi also put their arms around behind their bodies, turned the palms of their hands outwards and concealed their weapons when they recognized Freytag. They stood facing one another, looking at one another without surprise but with open disapproval – as if they had secretly reckoned on meeting each other and at the same time cursed such a meeting. Rethorn pointed with his thumb in the direction of the mess and said:

'Let us go in, in half an hour we shall have dealt with them. It won't take longer.'

'If I were you I should go below,' said Freytag.

'If you don't want to join in, then let us go ahead,' said Rethorn. 'You can keep right out of it, we'll see to it ourselves.'

'Go down below,' said Freytag.

'Have you forgotten who is on the ship?'

'I have forgotten nothing.'

'Two of them are asleep,' said Rethorn. 'Only the idiot is awake and he is sitting under the ventilator, he couldn't be in a better position.'

'You heard what I said.'

'Why are you against it?' said Rethorn.

'Go below, I have no wish to have Gombert sew one of you up in sailcloth tomorrow.'

'Then – '

'We'll try it,' said Rethorn.

'But not on this ship,' said Freytag, 'not so long as I'm captain.'

He fell silent, astonished at what he had said, for in all the years in which he had been master of a ship he had never before had to threaten with his position on board, and from Rethorn's demeanor, and also from the demeanor of the others, who were eying him with skeptical amazement, he observed immediately that something had happened that he had not intended.

'Away with you,' he said. 'Take the blackjacks to bed with you.'

'I should take them to the tool cupboard,' a voice said unexpectedly. 'That's the proper place for them and not in bed.'

In the open door of the mess stood Dr Caspary, behind him, the sawed-off shotgun at his hip, Eugen Kuhl, who grinned his agreement and, after Dr Caspary had strolled out smiling, shut the door from the inside.

'Is anything wrong on deck?' cried Zumpe from the lookout.

'Nothing,' replied Dr Caspary. 'We're just establishing the disadvantage of night work.'

'Come,' said Rethorn, and he, Philippi, and Soltow went astern, each of them holding one arm stiffly down, so that it looked as if each of them had an artificial arm. Dr Caspary gazed after them cheerfully until they had disappeared, then he turned to Freytag and said: 'I was sound asleep, but their voices woke me.'

'I'm sorry about that,' said Freytag.

'Oh,' said Dr Caspary, 'that is something I found out very early. Precisely in those places where you imagine you are safe from noise – on land, on the water, on an island – it torments you most of all, though in a different manner. Here the individual sound rules, and a certain voice is quite enough to stir up a brainstorm.'

'I must go up on the bridge,' said Freytag.

'May I go with you?'

'I can't prevent you.'

'That's right,' said Dr Caspary. 'It sounds odd, but it's perfectly true.'

They climbed up to the bridge and Freytag opened a

small cabin whose walls were covered with charts and which contained only a wide table and a chair. The table was covered with a thick plate of glass under which there also lay a chart. In a bookcase behind and to one side of the chair stood books and on the top a notebook with stiff cardboard covers.

Dr Caspary pulled out the notebook, opened it, walked over to the electric light, and began to skim through it.

'Your logbook?' he asked.

'Yes,' said Freytag.

'It contains everything that happens on board, doesn't it?'

'Everything.'

'Terrible,' said Dr Caspary. 'Time on a ship must be terrible, if every day and event is recorded like that. Everything can be looked up, no gap, no secret. Here life becomes nothing but a piece of bookkeeping.'

'It has its advantages,' said Freytag.

'Oh,' said Dr Caspary, 'I have always tried to forget particular events, to wipe them out. I should have liked to begin each day by wiping away all trace of the one before; for what can we expect of a new day that still stands in the shadow of the old one?'

'A settling of accounts,' said Freytag.

'Very good,' said Dr Caspary smiling, and after a pause and as he turned the pages towards the last entry: 'I suppose we have also had the honor of appearing in your book.'

'Not yet,' said Freytag.

'Were you just going to make good the omission?'

'I am bound to. Everything that happens on board has to be entered in the log.'

Dr Caspary nodded sorrowfully, tapped with his index finger on the cardboard cover of the logbook and said: 'Those are the traps we don't notice: the traps of order.

We have become as terribly used to them as your ship has become used to the chain.'

'Now I have to work,' said Freytag.

'I know,' said Dr Caspary, 'you want to keep on the heels of events. But how would it be if you didn't mention our visit, if you left a blank space, so that later it would be impossible for anyone to decide what really happened? You should try it, you should simply leave everything out: how you picked us up, what the weather was like, what happened on board – let nothing be mentioned in your bookkeeping, and all at once your ship would have a secret, a dark spot. Later, people would say: "Around that time, on the lightship, shortly before the winter storms – " but nobody would know anything precise.'

'Give me the logbook,' said Freytag.

'And then?'

'Everything that happens on board has to be entered in it.'

'Including our visit?'

'Yes,' said Freytag, 'everything.'

'But we're not interested in being mentioned. Although I should like to see what marks you would give us, we attach no value to being imprisoned in your book. I'm sure we have understood one another.'

'Give me the book,' said Freytag.

Dr Caspary laid the book on the table and began to polish the signet ring on his hip with limp, mechanical movements and equally mechanically to raise the hand with the ring on it to the naked electric-light bulb from time to time. As he did so, he watched Freytag pick up the logbook, open it, leaf through it and finally snap it shut and put it back on the shelf without having made an entry in it.

'We have understood one another, Captain,' said Dr Caspary. 'There is probably no one on board with whom I can achieve such understanding as with you.'

It sounded very convincing, it sounded like a confession, and Freytag raised his face in surprise and looked at the man expectantly, and for a moment he imagined he could see that Dr Caspary was prepared to explain or confide something to him, but then the masklike smile appeared on his features again, silently and abruptly, as the surface of the sea changes, and Freytag stood up and walked out onto the bridge.

'May I join you?' said Dr Caspary.

'I can't prevent you,' said Freytag.

Beneath the starless blackness of the horizon hung the lights of an approaching ship, drifted slowly upwards, rose like the periscope of a surfacing submarine, laboriously, steadily, so that it looked as if the ship were rising from the bottom of the sea. The flashing beam of the lightship flickered towards it like a pointing arm, went out and flared up again.

'Can they see us from over there?' asked Dr Caspary.

'We are the seamark by which they are steering,' said Freytag. 'They can see us at a distance of fifteen nautical miles.'

'Then they are shaping their course by us.'

'They are shaping their course by the ship's beacon,' said Freytag.

'Very good,' said Dr Caspary. 'I understand what you mean. The others shape their course by the signal you give. It's all the same to them who is on board the lightship, so long as they receive your signal that determines their course. So long as the light is flashing from this masthead the men on the other ships will be satisfied, because they imagine that then there is order at sea. Is that it?'

'Yes,' said Freytag, 'more or less.'

'So the others don't care who gives them the signal?'

'They receive the signal which they need,' said Freytag,

'which will bring them past the shoals to the harbor – the rest doesn't concern them.'

'Good,' said Dr Caspary. 'Then it would make no difference to the others if they received the signal from my men instead of from yours.'

'What are you plotting?'

'Nothing. I'm only trying to get to the bottom of things; I'm trying to figure out the significance of the fact that the others expect the signal from your lightship and nothing else. It's all the same to them who looks after the signal.'

'So long as the course is correct and they are safe, it's all the same to them.'

'And if suddenly it is no longer correct, if the signal unexpectedly changes, secretly, unannounced – what will the others do then? Probably what they are used to: they will spot the signal, will accept it and, without slowing down, will run onto the sandbanks. Not until the keel is firmly wedged will they realize that they have omitted something – omitted to concern themselves about who was giving them the signal.'

'That's what we are here for,' said Freytag, 'and the men out there know that they can rely on us. Up to now we have always brought them in safely.'

'But you're no longer alone on board,' said Dr Caspary.

'I've noticed that,' said Freytag.

'But the men out there know nothing about that,' said Dr Caspary, indicating the ship that was coming closer, brightly lit and with a glimmering bow wash, to pass them at an angle.

'We have them in the palm of our hand and we needn't do much to send them on the shoals. They're bound to act upon the signals we send them?'

'Yes,' said Freytag, 'they would act upon them.'

'That's all I wanted to know, Captain. Will you have a cigarette?'

46

Freytag pointed with his finger at the cold cigarette which he held between his lips, shook his head and raised the night glasses to his eyes and looked across at the ship. It was a passenger steamer with its midships lit up and two rows of lit-up portholes that glided through the darkness like chains of little moons, gentle and solemn. The steamer had passed the wreck-buoy and was now running abeam, and Freytag recognized the golden crossed keys on the funnel, the sign of the shipping company; he recognized shadows moving behind the portholes, a woman combing her hair, men hauling a tarpaulin from the forward hatch, and he pictured what would happen on the steamer if the keel slid grating into the sand, if a shudder ran through the ship as the screw, lashing like the caudal fin of a strangled whale, drove it with a furious effort deeper and deeper into the tenacious bottom; he imagined that he could hear the cries, the footsteps on the gangways, when the lights went out, and then the cracking of glass, timber, and crockery and the roar from the engine room, from which they would report a severe leak. He lowered the glasses again, put them in the case and turned around to Dr Caspary.

'So long as we are on board,' he said, 'the others can rely on us.'

'I'm glad you're convinced of that,' said Dr Caspary. 'Then you will see to it that there is no change and that our boat gets repaired.'

Freytag closed his eyes, rested his hands on the wet railing of the bridge, stood in silence as though laboring under the effects of exertion, and said after a while: 'Whatever happens aboard this ship, she will never leave her position. Anything else may happen but not that. The ship stays here.'

'It is in your hands,' said Dr Caspary.

Freytag did not reply, he bent down over the railing of the bridge and looked down at the deck, where a figure

47

was moving, sighing, with shuffling steps; the figure –
Freytag recognized it as the man with the harelip – passed
below him to the accommodation ladder, stood still for a
second, swung himself over the side, and slowly went
down out of sight; then the boat, which was attached by
the painter, scraped against the side of the ship with a
booming noise, the sound of a man jumping came up to
the bridge, and Freytag knew that at that moment there
were only two of them on the lightship, Dr Caspary
beside him and Eddie in the messroom.

'That was Eugen,' said Dr Caspary. 'He has climbed
down into the boat to see to something,' and as Freytag
looked at him with his head on one side: 'Now there are
only two of us on board; I imagine you were just thinking
about that, Captain.'

'Yes, I was thinking about that,' said Freytag.

'And have you made up your mind?'

'To do what?'

'I am unarmed,' said Dr Caspary. 'I hate going around
with my pockets full; besides, I'm not very strong and I
was never a fighter. In all my life I have never engaged
in physical combat, not even as a boy in the school
playground.'

'Am I supposed to feel sorry for you on that account?'
asked Freytag. 'Or what do you expect?'

'I expect you to react like a man who does bookkeeping
every day on this ship.'

'What do you mean by that?'

'You could now arrange for there to be only one of us
left on board: Eddie in the messroom.'

'Listen,' said Freytag, 'I have met a great many men in
my life, I have seen them rise and become something
and fall, and I have understood everything about them,
including the way they died; but I can't understand you.
You are the first man who has had me baffled. You don't
48

fit together with the other two. You're a case all by yourself.'

'That's correct,' said Dr Caspary. 'And it has always been my ambition to be a case all by myself. I have always made an effort to achieve that.'

'And you have succeeded,' said Freytag, and he suddenly reached for the glasses and looked aft, where a long line of rectangular scraps of paper were floating on the iron-gray sea, rocking to and fro, shimmering dimly in the early light and drifting lethargically along just beneath the surface towards the shore, like scraps of paper dropped on a paper chase. When the lightship's beacon flared up, the water above the pieces of paper flashed; a few of them were circling around behind the stern in the whirlpools produced by the current, and of the pieces that were farthest away several had become waterlogged, were sinking, and as they sank drifted on towards the shore, and in the darkness of the depths they glimmered like floating dead fish. The rocking trail of scraps of paper stretched far out into the light that was breaking over the sea, and Freytag followed it through the glasses, forward and back, forward and back; then, without lowering the glasses, he glanced out of the corner of his eye at Dr Caspary and saw that he was leaning against the wall out of the wind and also watching the rocking trail of paper.

'Do you see that?' asked Freytag.

'Yes,' said Dr Caspary.

'What is it?'

'Letters. My friends brought a whole bag of letters into the boat. I guess Eugen must be sitting down below and dispatching them like this.'

'If the wind doesn't turn they may cover the beach by tomorrow,' said Freytag. 'A few of them will reach it anyhow,' and he thought of what Rethorn had told him, about the postman whom one of them had shot and whose mailbag had disappeared; and he thought that the first person to find the letters on the beach was bound to become suspicious enough to broadcast his discovery, whereupon the people on land would decide to send search parties over the bay.

'You're right,' said Dr Caspary – and Freytag started as Caspary once more guessed his thoughts – 'if the wind and the current don't change, the beach will be covered with letters tomorrow morning, and probably the first person to find them will see to it that a search is made for the sender.'

Dr Caspary hurriedly left the bridge, and this time Freytag followed him; they walked forward to the accommodation ladder, bent over the rail and saw the giant sitting on the bottom of the boat, the sawed-off shotgun beside him and between his legs a pile of parcels and letters, which he picked up one by one from the top, tore open, pulled apart with a single movement like a pay envelope, and after feeling inside with his thumb and index finger sent them sailing overboard with a flick of the wrist. He merely groped about inside some envelopes, others he tore right open, unfolded letters, twisted and turned them in his hand, and once he interrupted his activities to push something into his breast pocket. Freytag couldn't make out what it was that the man down there had slipped into his pocket, but he knew that Eugen was looking for banknotes and that he had found at least one.

Dr Caspary watched him for a while before he called out to him and politely persuaded him not to throw any more letters into the water. 'It isn't good, Eugen,' he said. 'Over there on the land they will find the letters and open them to trace the sender, and they will only have to follow the floating letters to find their way here.' Eugen listened attentively and Dr Caspary talked down to him very politely, paying him compliments – 'a man like you will quickly see that' – until the giant nodded in agreement, raked the parcels and letters into a mailbag and clambered up again with bag and shotgun aboard the lightship, where he handed the letters to Dr Caspary.

'It may look as though we mean to open a post office,' said Dr Caspary, 'but you have nothing to fear, Captain: we have no intention of installing a counter here on board. Besides, we lack the special rubber stamp required for the purpose.'

'You will have to pay for that,' said Freytag. 'All the people who wrote those letters and should have received them will one day make their claims.'

'You are mistaken,' said Dr Caspary. 'Nobody can make claims on the Post Office; what has once been placed in its care cannot be demanded back. My friend knows that.'

He fell silent, because a shadow hopped along the deck and between the men's legs, so that they instinctively moved apart, and immediately afterwards they heard Gombert's footsteps and his coaxing voice, 'Edith,' he called out, 'come, Edith, come,' and as he approached in a crouching position, snapping his fingers, the rook hopped around the men's feet with one of its limply dangling, clipped wings brushing along the deck.

'Come, Edith, come,' cajoled Gombert, and Eugen repeated like an echo 'Come, come,' and pushed the rook with the sawed-off barrel of the shotgun.

'*Corvus frugilegus,*' said Dr Caspary.

'Careful,' cried Gombert, 'don't tread on her wings.'

The rook squatted down between the giant's parallel feet, its graphite-colored beak with the split at the tip slightly open and its purple-glinting plumage ruffled.

'Careful,' Freytag too said now. 'It's a valuable rook, it can talk.'

'The value of speech depends upon the text,' said Dr Caspary.

'What can you say, then?' asked the giant. 'Can you recite the hymn book or tell a fairy story? Come on, start, whisper something in my ear.'

'I'm sure she knows the Lighthouse Table,' said Dr Caspary.

'Come, Edith, come,' said Gombert coaxingly.

Eugen bent down, slowly lowered one hand, the fingers of which were outspread like a pair of tongs, as though he meant to plunge it onto the rook's head like a fork, but before he touched it the bird stretched, snapped upwards and dug its split beak into the ball of the man's thumb; the giant recoiled with the shock and in so doing pulled the rook up into the air, its beak firmly gripping his hand. The rook fell to the deck again with a thud, stretched its neck in a swallowing movement and, after shaking itself vigorously, sat calmly where it was.

Eugen looked at his bleeding hand, pressed and felt it in astonishment, and all at once his yellow goat's eyes closed to a slit, his hand darted down so fast this time that the rook ducked like a clutched chicken. He seized it by the neck and threw it overboard. The clipped wings flapped fast in a hopeless attempt at flight, and there was another flapping sound as the feathered body struck the water. The rook did not go under, the outspread wings broke its fall and now began to beat desperately, while the claws paddled across the water in wild running movements like the little feet of a coot that is trying to rise up into the air but cannot, because its body is too heavy. A narrow trail of foam and bubbles appeared where the rook moved over the surface of the water, beating its wings and paddling with its feet, a trail that first led straight away from the ship, then ran around in a curve and ended in ever-narrowing circles; finally only one wing was beating.

'It doesn't even call for help,' said Dr Caspary.

The man with the harelip raised his gun and fired; the

charge of small shot smashed into the body of the rook and onto the water and flung up a shallow fountain of spray. The bird's wing stretched out, dipped under the water and hung down limply.

'She couldn't think of anything else to say,' said Eugen, reloaded the shotgun, turned in a flash to face Gombert and calmly watched him coming towards him with his hands open and held a little away out in front of him.

'Take care,' cried Freytag.

'Come, Edith, come, ' said the giant, imitating Gombert's voice.

'Stay where you are,' said Freytag.

'Come,' said the giant, 'come quite close.'

He held the sawed-off shotgun to his hip, the barrel pointing at Gombert's abdomen, and his eyes narrowed.

'Go back, Gombert,' said Freytag.

'Another six feet,' said Eugen, tilting his head back; the tip of his tongue ran once over his split lip, his bleeding hand took hold of the barrel to support it from underneath.

'Gombert!' cried Freytag sharply.

Gombert came to a stop and helplessly lowered his arms; a twitch ran through his pendulous cheeks. He looked at the barrel of the gun, turned around and went to the rail and looked down at the black body of the rook floating limply in the swell and drifting slowly aft like the shimmering chain of letters.

'I'm afraid, Captain,' said Dr Caspary, 'it's time for us to leave; my friends are already impatient. See to it that our boat is finished and remember that we have set ourselves a time limit. Anything we can save counts as a gain.'

The fogbank hung over the long bay: at midday, as the mist moved across from the islands towards the ship the water became smooth and marble-black, the lightship's bow cast a steep, flaming-red silhouette, silence lay upon the sea and the sun hung dull and rayless above the fogbank. The high-pitched ping-pong of a small hammer echoed over the ship, and at regular intervals the warning howl of the fog siren resounded from the bridge, penetrated the fluid whiteness and ran across the bay in echoless vibrations. The fog lay over the ship like a bell, like a shallow dome, ceaselessly changing shape, hiding the light tower and the masts, drifting around the superstructure and billowing down onto the water.

Freytag stood on the bridge, listening to the chugging of the engine of a ship that had come closer and closer, had run for a while abeam and was now moving off towards the open sea, without Zumpe, who was on fog lookout at the bow, having seen the ship. The chugging, grinding sound grew fainter, existed only as a slight hum, then as a memory, till finally it disappeared.

'She has gone,' said Freytag in a low voice.

Behind him, Philippi stepped out of the chartroom, as though he had been waiting for this cue. Nonchalantly he flicked a cigarette butt into the water, nonchalantly he came and stood beside Freytag and put his hands in his pockets and lowered his face.

'We're finished,' said Freytag. 'That's all I wanted you for: transmit nothing but your reports, sign off as you always sign off, and do nothing to arouse the suspicions of the Coast Guard Office. Nothing special has happened on board.'

'If I listen to you and shut my eyes I might almost believe that,' said Philippi.

'I know what I have to do,' said Freytag.

'Hearty congratulations,' said Philippi.

'Go now and send out your reports.'

'But first I must ask you for a signature.'

'What for? In the past you have signed all reports yourself.'

'I didn't have to shut my eyes when I transmitted them.'

'I'll sign,' said Freytag.

Philippi nodded and left the bridge without a word of farewell, a mocking smile on his hawk's face; the roller door of the wireless cabin flew open with a cracking sound, was shut with the same violence, and Freytag went into the chartroom, sat down at the table and leaned his body forward on the glass tabletop. He felt the glass pressing coldly against his cheek and temple, felt his breath on the back of his hand, and as he listened to the deep howl of the fog siren he was overcome by a sensation of shivering exhaustion. He stood up, opened the door and put it on the hook, then he laid his body forward over the table again, his arms crossed under his chest, and tried to sleep.

He didn't go to sleep. He opened his eyes and lay awake and looked at the gnarled joints of his fingers, at the coppery glint that lay over the soft hairs on the back of his hand, at the thick slab of glass on which a funnel-shaped patch of condensation formed as he breathed, and he thought of the old white city down in the Aegean. He was surprised to find himself thinking about it, was startled, because he had long ago imagined that it had vanished from his memory, but now it extended like a terrace in front of the foothills and was visible in all its brutal brightness: the town in which the roots of his memory would forever lie. Shouts came up to him from the accommodation ladder, a sharp draft as though from a chain of swiftly flying ducks swept across the ship. He thought of the town that was conquering the naked mountain, sending its cottages higher and higher till they reached the violet shadows under the peak, and he saw their reflection on the pale-green water: the squat, dazzling church, the white cottages with the roof gardens on which washing hung out to dry; the sheds; the protective arm of the pier bent at an angle to the sea; and he imagined that he could hear the thunder of the train that passed through the ravine into the back country. And while he imagined he was hearing it, a footstep approached the chartroom, a footstep that seemed to come from desperately far away, that fell and fell and approached with unbearable slowness, as if it hesitated to reach its goal, or as if it lacked strength or certainty: hard and echoless on deck, shuffling in the port gangway, then resolute on the iron companion ladder – thus it came closer, and Freytag thought of the old white town and heard the tormenting footstep, but he remained lying over the cold glass slab on top of the chart table until the footstep echoed on the bridge. Wearily, he straightened up and looked at the open door. In the doorway stood Fred.

'Ah,' said Freytag, 'it's you. It sounded as though you had come all the way from the shore and would never manage to get here.'

The boy didn't answer; he cast a glance of silent hostility at the old man, came into the chartroom and unhooked the door and shut it.

'Won't you sit down?' asked Freytag.

'I've rarely been so glad to stand,' said Fred.

Freytag smiled and made the cold cigarette wag in the corner of his mouth.

'Can I help you?' he asked.

'I don't need your help,' said Fred. 'I want to tell you something.'

'I know,' said Freytag, 'I reckoned on that.'

'Something I have been wanting to tell you for a long time.'

'Yes, I know. You have waited a long time for this moment and now you think it has come.'

'I had to talk to you sometime.'

'Yes.'

'We haven't much to talk about. I only want to tell you that now I believe what they said about you at the time and still say about you now. Now everything is clear to me. To begin with, I didn't believe it and again and again I tried to forget what they said, but now I know that it's all true.'

'What's true?' asked Freytag.

'That you left Natzmer in the lurch that time. You did nothing to get him out and take him away; you went back on board without him, because – '

'Because?'

'You're a coward,' said Fred. 'You left Natzmer in the lurch because you were afraid something might happen to you; yes, that's right, now I know. You did nothing to bring him back, just as you now do nothing, because the others are armed.'

'Then you know more than I do,' said Freytag, 'and I was there.'

'One doesn't have to be there in order to know.'

'And what is it you know?'

'I've heard the whole story often enough,' said Fred, 'and the part you played in the story – at the time you were master of the *Klintje*.'

'We were carrying grain,' said Freytag, 'twelve hundred tons of wheat, and we were cruising among the islands down in the Aegean.'

'When you came back on board without Natzmer the whole crew wanted to go ashore and fetch him, but you were against it, and you sailed without him.'

'Is that what they say?' asked Freytag with a resigned smile.

'I know that's how it was,' said Fred. 'You had been cruising about for a long time off the town, and when you tied up they met you with stones and clubs with nails stuck in them. None of you dared go ashore, you didn't dare either, but when you were ordered to call at the police station you had to leave the ship, secretly, in the early morning, and you took Natzmer with you and Lubisch, your mate.'

The boy stopped in the expectation that the old man would say something, would correct him, he looked at him challengingly, with open contempt, but Freytag sat there in an attitude of apathetic listening, said nothing and nodded imperceptibly, and the boy went on: 'You three went ashore – that's right, isn't it? – before dawn, before they had gathered by the ship with stones and clubs; it was far too early, the police station was still shut, and you intended to hide near the police station and wait till it opened. Go ahead and tell me if there's anything I haven't got right; I want you to hear everything I know, so that things are clear between us. You crept to the police station, but there was no place to hide nearby, as you had expected; instead, the others were waiting for you, they caught you and took you to the ravine; tell me if anything isn't right. There in the ravine they tied Natzmer up and poured sea water down his throat; he lay on the rock in the sun, for two days, and you were there the whole time and saw his hunger and heard him calling out to you. After two days they brought you and

58

Lubisch back, the ship had put out and anchored in the roads, and they pointed to the ship, threw you in the water and told you to swim out. You swam out, but Lubisch dived and tried to go straight back to the land and into the ravine where Natzmer still lay tied up. Lubisch went on trying until they shot at him and struck him in the shoulder as he swam; just tell me if anything isn't right. And when the whole crew wanted to go ashore and fetch Natzmer you prevented them; you ordered them to weigh anchor, you left Natzmer in the lurch, because you were afraid of their guns. You're a coward.'

Fred looked intently at his father, undismayed by what he had said; he expected something, although he didn't know how it would express itself: gruff rebuttal or bitter recrimination or anger; he anticipated that his father would automatically rise to his own defense, would put forward a series of good reasons for his actions, but nothing happened, he saw him merely sitting there apathetically, bent, his gnarled fingers on the glass plate, and he involuntarily took a step towards him, leaned forward and asked:

'Did you hear everything I said? I'm through; I have nothing more to say, there's nothing more anyone could say.'

Freytag moved his lips, as though to make sure before speaking that what he was going to say would also be audible; then he asked: 'Is that what they say?'

'Yes,' said Fred, 'that's what people say; I've been hearing it for years, from Natzmer's son, from Elke Lubisch, and every time I saw Lubisch himself sitting there with his stiff arm I thought about it, and I never went past his house when he was sitting on the bench.'

'You heard it from him,' said Freytag.

'I heard it from everyone,' said Fred. 'Everyone in my class knew it.'

'Did you ask them?'

'They asked me.'

'And you told them what you had learned from those who weren't there?'

'That was enough,' said Fred.

'Maybe,' said Freytag. 'Perhaps it is enough to learn the truth in small amounts. He who knows half knows something.'

'I had no further need to ask you,' said Fred.

'Lubisch was there too,' said Freytag. 'You could have asked him when he was sitting on the bench outside his house, you needn't have avoided him.'

'He would have told me the same story,' said Fred.

'He can't tell you the same story, no one can tell the same story as someone else has already told; the one Lubisch would have told you would have been quite different, because he was there.'

'He would only have confirmed what I already knew, and I was afraid of that confirmation.'

'No,' said Freytag, 'Lubisch would have begun differently from you and ended differently. He would have told you that we had twelve hundred tons of wheat on board when we sailed down with the *Klintje*, twelve hundred tons destined for the hunger zone. Lubisch knew that, and he also knew that shortly before we reached port we received new orders from the shipping company to cruise around out of sight of the port and wait. You didn't have to ask me to learn that; Lubisch would have told you too, and from him you would also have heard that we had a Greek on board who came from the hunger zone of the island; we called him Kaxi, because no one could remember his name, which sounded something like that. Kaxi was the strongest man on board, a man who worked as I have never seen anybody work, and when we were loading wheat for his island he refused to go off duty and worked until the whole cargo was on board.'

'This Greek has nothing to do with it,' said Fred.

'Just wait,' said Freytag. 'If you had asked Lubisch you would know how much Kaxi had to do with it; because when we changed course, didn't take the wheat ashore, but had to cruise about among the islands, he came to me and asked me to put in at the port. I told him that I had orders from the company to cruise, and he said the company only wanted to wait until the price of wheat had risen still higher. I could do nothing to help him.

'We cruised for several days, and one evening the Greek seemed to have gone mad; he came to me and asked me if I would put in at the port if he succeeded in beating the whole crew in single combat – he had simply gone mad at the thought of his people. And Lubisch would have told you that I announced Kaxi's proposal in the mess and that everyone was in favour of it, because nothing is so dreary as cruising about and waiting for fresh orders.

'We had sunshine and a calm sea, mats were spread out on the middle deck, Natzmer was elected referee, yes, and in the evenings, when it grew cooler, members of the crew came forward to wrestle with the Greek. He beat all those who came forward, and when I was the only one left I knew that our agreement amounted to a promise and that I should have to keep this promise if I didn't succeed in getting the better of him.'

'Did you beat him?' asked Fred.

'I don't know,' said Freytag. 'Lubisch would have told you that almost the whole crew was on deck when I entered the ring against him. First I had him, then he sat astride me and tried to pull apart my hands, with which I was throttling him, and when he had succeeded I lifted him up in the air and rolled over, then I got him in a half Nelson, but he managed to free himself by exerting such a pull with his neck and shoulder that I thought he would tear out my arm. Then, when I had him in a leg scissors and was constricting his carotid artery, something happened which all the crew saw and which Lubisch saw too: Kaxi was lying half on top of me so that it looked as though he might crush me, and at this moment Natzmer struck. I didn't see it, but Lubisch saw Natzmer hit the Greek on the back of the neck with a spar; I wasn't at all pleased, although I knew that the first mate was only trying to help me. The Greek's resistance ceased immediately, he lay face down on the mat, and three of us had to carry him below and bring him around with a bucket of sea water. Next morning, when the coast hove into view for a short time, the Greek jumped overboard.'

'Did he reach land?'

'Yes,' said Freytag, 'and twenty-four hours later we received orders to put into port and discharge our cargo; and we were greeted as you said: with stones and clubs with nails stuck in them. Kaxi had got to the town before us, and they knew that we had been cruising about with the wheat on board; they knew everything – as Lubisch would have confirmed if you hadn't avoided him, and from him you could also have heard that the people on the island would have liked to tip our wheat into the sea, because to them it was dirty wheat. If the police hadn't sent armed men to the pier not a bushel of the cargo would have reached land, but I must tell you – and Lubisch would have mentioned it too – that the men from the police station secretly thought just like the others, to them too it was dirty wheat that was being unloaded, and they didn't speak to us and turned their backs on us while they kept guard over the unloading. All of us distrusted them. And after the cargo had been discharged we were requested to report to the police station – Natzmer, Lubisch, and I; they set a time in the morning, although they could see that in the morning we wouldn't be able to take two steps over the pier without

62

being bombarded with stones and beaten with nail-studded clubs, and so we went ashore before dawn, before the town was awake and the people had gathered by the ship. Today I don't believe the order came from the police station, even if a policeman brought it, because later the police station showed no interest in us, although they should have known what had happened. Lubisch was there when the three of us went ashore and in the street in which the police station stood we were forced by armed men to get into a truck that took us out to the ravine where there were no houses. Above the railway embankment the road came to an end, the truck stopped, and when we jumped out, Kaxi was standing there with a spar in his hand. He returned Natzmer's blow without saying a word; at a sign from him they tied up the mate, poured sea water down his throat and laid him on the rocks in the sun. There he lay for two days and a night, and we sat with the others in a semicircle around him, eating and drinking nothing all that time – they didn't eat or drink anything themselves either – and if we moved they reached for their old-fashioned revolvers that lay at their feet. Neither they nor we spoke during those two days and one night, no one was allowed to go away – if anyone had to relieve himself he had to do so on the spot where he was sitting. No, we didn't hear a word; all we heard was the thunder of the railway that passed through the ravine in the evenings, and the cries of the birds of prey circling high above the ravine, nothing else. They forced us to sit there and look at Natzmer who lay stretched out in his bonds on the hot rocks – Lubisch was beside me and he would have told you that if you had asked him. And if he had been able to endure the memory you would now know that he did no more than I: sat there and said nothing, and perhaps thought of the blow with which Natzmer knocked out the Greek at a moment when my position was better than he thought.

I'm only telling you what Lubisch would have had to tell you if his memory hasn't sprung a leak. He would have told you that on the second night we were made to get into a truck – he and I, not Natzmer – that they drove us back into the town and then out along the coast road to the cliffs, where they drove us down the slope and showed us the lights of the *Klintje*, which had put to sea and was anchored out in the roads. Kaxi was no longer there. The men who had accompanied us threw us from the cliffs into the water and stood up above with their old-fashioned revolvers and watched us swimming. Lubisch swam behind me, and after we were so far from land that they could no longer hear us, he talked about swimming to land and going back to the ravine to look for Natzmer, but I knew that they were standing up above on the cliffs and only waiting for that. I refused to do it. And I thought he had given up the idea, until I suddenly noticed that he was no longer swimming behind me, and then I heard the shots, heard his cry; and I turned around and dived for him, while they shot at us. We were swimming for over three hours. When we got on board Lubisch was unconscious.'

'Lubisch had a try,' said Fred.

'Yes,' said Freytag, 'and later on board they also wanted to have a try, they wanted to go ashore together and fetch Natzmer, although we had new orders to go to Rotterdam. A few even thought the police would help look for Natzmer – the same people who would rather have carried nail-studded clubs than the rifles with which they were supposed to protect us. We had no weapons, and in those days too I saw no use in trying to argue with the muzzle of a revolver. I put the whole thing in the hands of the company and our agent – I could do no more; because the ship had new orders and I wanted to bring the crew back.'

64

'But Natzmer didn't come back,' said Fred. 'The company filled in forms, and the agent took the forms to the police station, and all that was just as much good as if the forms had been thrown overboard.'

'Natzmer was past help. You can always get into a situation in which there is nothing you can do except fill in forms and pass them on, although you know perfectly well that you would do just as much good by throwing them overboard.'

'That's just like you,' said Fred. 'You took no risks and weren't prepared to take any risks. Before you try anything you ask for guarantees, and you would never do anything against a criminal until he had given you his word of honor that his ammunition had run out; only then would your moment have arrived.'

'Clever of you to think that out,' said Freytag.

'It's right,' said Fred. 'Now I know.'

'You know nothing,' said Freytag. 'So long as you imagine that the only course open to an unarmed man is to argue with gun muzzles I don't give a damn for what you know. I'll tell you something, lad. I have never been a hero and I don't want to become a martyr; both of those types have always seemed very suspect to me: they died too easily and even in death they were still certain of their cause – too certain, I think, and that is no solution. I have known men who died in order to settle something. They settled nothing, they left everything behind. Their death helped them but nobody else. A man with no weapons and no power still has more chance than a dead man, and I often think that behind this desire to offer oneself at any price to the muzzle of a gun lies the worst egotism.'

'That doesn't interest me,' said Fred. 'I only want to know one thing: why did you send Rethorn and the others away when they wanted to capture those three?'

'I have just told you.'

'And suppose they had brought it off?'

'Then today Gombert would be sewing them up in sailcloth; that's what they would have brought off.'

'So you won't take any steps against them?'

'I want the ship to complete her last watch and everyone to be on board when we return to port – nothing more; and that is why nothing will be done aboard this ship without my consent.'

'That's all,' said Fred. 'I've finished.'

'I expected that,' said Freytag.

'Then you are spared being surprised.'

'Someone on board is going to be surprised,' said Freytag with a resigned smile, and he stood up as the boy left the chartroom, followed him onto the bridge, clambered down the companion ladder after him, and followed him with his eyes as he walked through the fog to the bows – swiftly, erect, with tapping, echoless steps; stopped and waited till he had vanished in a lethargically drifting mist, and then strolled to the accommodation ladder and leaned over the rail.

The line to which they had attached the damaged boat hung slackly in the water, swaying to and fro like the long, gray antenna of an insect, soundless, serpentine, as though palping the seaweed-covered hull of the ship. Freytag looked along the line in the direction in which the boat must lie in the fog and from which he had heard the ping-ping of the little hammer when he was with Philippi on the bridge. Now all was quiet, he could discern no shadow, no outline, and as far as he could see the line did not rise up out of the water to the bow of the boat. In a low voice he called down, called out Soltow's given name, but he received no answer. Nor did anyone appear on the deck of the lightship when he called out, and he looked suspiciously at the line swaying limply in the water and appearing to sink deeper and deeper, and suddenly swung himself onto the accommodation ladder and climbed down. He took hold of the line, slowly hauled in the slack, and waited for a tug that would announce the resistance of the boat; with a soft grating sound the line scraped along the hull towards him, long, far too long, so that even before he held the end in his hand he knew that something had happened to the damaged boat, and when the end did come – loose fibers, as though hacked through with a blow from an ax – he pulled it up and examined it and listened into the fog, as though he conjectured that the boat which had been cut loose from the line was still floating nearby. Then he took a swing and hurled the line out again and heard it fall on the water with a splash. *Rethorn*, he thought, *he and no one else cut the boat adrift, and even if Soltow did it, it must at least have been Rethorn's idea. He wanted to spring the trap and so he took away their boat. He will deny it, but it can only have been him. He has been against me from the very first day.* Freytag climbed up the ladder to the deck, where he turned around again and listened into the fogbank that lay over the ship and over the bay, and now he thought of Dr Caspary and the others and tried to picture how they would react when they noticed the disappearance of their boat. He imagined that he could see Dr Caspary standing there with his spotted sunglasses, mechanically polishing his chunky signet ring on his hip, and he imagined that he could hear his voice, that soft, clear voice which sounded so polite when it threatened. He walked slowly to the messroom.

He knocked, a broad face appeared behind a porthole, automatically, as the faces of the 'bobbing bastards' on the shooting range automatically appear above the parapet, a door was cautiously opened, the man with the harelip appeared in the crack, and with a vigorous nod of the head he invited Freytag to come in. Dr Caspary was sitting at the table playing solitaire; in one corner of the mess, on a row of chairs, Eddie was sleeping with the submachine gun by his head, so that he could have reached and fired it while still lying down. Eugen went back to his seat at the table, where an enamel mug of steaming coffee stood and from where he watched the solitaire with a grin.

Freytag saw at once that they were his cards with which Dr Caspary was playing, and he also saw that the little glass-fronted cupboard in which he kept his cards was standing open.

'It isn't going to come out,' said Dr Caspary after a while, 'no, it's not. But what would be the sense of a game in which there was no chance of disappointment?'

'I must speak to you,' said Freytag.

'Is our boat ready?'

'No.'

Dr Caspary calmly swept the cards together, tapped them into a neat pack and thrust the pack into a box. 'I'm ready,' he said.

'You have no chance left of getting off this ship,' said Freytag.

'May I ask upon what your supposition rests?'

'Your boat has gone,' said Freytag. 'Someone has cut it adrift.'

'I thought your men were going to repair it; Eugen thought the same, didn't you, Eugen?'

'It is drifting in the fog,' said Freytag, 'and now it would be hopeless to search for the boat. We shouldn't find it.'

'You look as though you were worried about it, Captain.'

'I thought it proper to tell you.'

'I appreciate that greatly, but I was prepared for it. In fact I expected it to happen sooner.'

Freytag turned around in surprise, his eyes ran through the mess, as though he hoped somewhere to find a sign, an explanation for Dr Caspary's imperturbability, and he twisted his handkerchief around his hand and stretched the material with the pressure of his fingers.

'I don't know whether your boat is drifting towards the shore or out with the current.'

'It doesn't matter what happens to a boat that one no longer possesses,' said Dr Caspary.

'You were dependent on that boat,' said Freytag.

'But we had retained the right to choose.'

'You have no possibility left of getting off this ship.'

'Appearances speak against that, Captain. You have overlooked your boat, and you haven't considered that the ship itself, your lightship, can if needs be sail, even if it was only built for the chain.'

'I have already told you that this ship will never leave its position as long as I am on board.'

'And if you now had to give advice – what would you advise us?'

'Give up,' said Freytag. 'Give yourselves up. Even if you still had the boat, your chance of getting to Faaborg or anywhere else has grown so slim that it's not worth trying, and it is growing slimmer hour by hour.'

'You see, Captain, we differ on this point: you attach no value to uncertainty, and I don't attach much value to certainty: the slimmer our chances are in your eyes, the readier I am to bank on them. Certain experiences of mine support this view. I once had a smuggler among my clients who carried on his onerous trade during the war; he always conscientiously chose sectors of the front where there was the heaviest harassing fire. He always got through, whereas his partner, who preferred quiet sectors, was shot by a nervous outpost. I believe we have understood one another as we did before, and now you will not expect us to abandon a chance which is precious precisely because it is so slight. I hope you will have your boat repaired immediately and will place it at our disposal cheaply.'

Freytag took the cold cigarette out of his mouth, crushed it, and rubbed it to pieces between his fingers and then asked:

'Were you a lawyer?'

'Among other things I am a lawyer,' said Dr Caspary and made Freytag a curious, ironic bow.

Gombert was sitting in the bow of the boat, which was suspended from the davits, watching the nighttime storm over the coast: the harsh gashes of the lightning that flickered in the darkness like mineral veins, the deep black of the horizon, the pale violet at the edges of the clouds. The sea lay dull and lustreless under the retreating squall, even the foam of the waves did not shine but ran gray, mist-gray, across the waste of water, and the lightship's beacon seemed to have lost some of its sharpness, its hardness and strength, and blinked uncertainly out towards the bay like a torch with a flat battery. Gombert was sitting in the boat in his oilskins; he had let two furious squalls pass over him; he had observed the rising wind that had tautened the anchor chain and broken up the fogbank, and all the time he had held the heavy marlinspike in his hand like a clumsy dagger. Nobody on board knew that he was sitting there, patient and broad, the marlinspike in front of him, its thornlike shape fitting neatly into his hand; he had vaulted into the boat unnoticed immediately after supper, drawn his head in and sat in this position – his body bent, his legs stretched out – waiting. The ship dipped its bows in the sea, but without any water flowing over the deck; the light tower and the masts swayed, scratching short, upright writing in the sky as they swayed: standardized signals, code signals, which all masts at sea exchange with one another.

Every now and then Gombert cautiously raised his head above the gunwale and looked in the direction of the mess and over the middle deck, and when he heard a sound he rose to his knees and closed his fingers firmly around the wet metal of the marlinspike. He thought of the note which he had addressed to Eugen and pushed through the ventilator into the mess, shortly before supper, when Dr Caspary was aft with Freytag; he hadn't been able to make sure whether the giant had found it and read it at once, but he knew that the note had not stuck in the shaft but had fallen into the messroom. Gombert wasn't sure whether Eugen would keep what he had written to himself; perhaps he had immediately shown the note to Dr Caspary, in which case he was waiting in vain. But perhaps he had discussed the whole thing with his brother – a possibility with which Gombert had reckoned – and then the giant wouldn't come to the davits, but Eddie might come and find out whether what Gombert had written was true. He had written to Eugen that Dr Caspary intended to try to escape from the trap alone; a member of the crew, whom he had paid, was to help him lower the boat into the water. As soon as Dr Caspary left the mess, Eugen should not follow him, but come straight to the boat and wait. Gombert only hoped that the distrust among them was great enough.

For four hours he sat in the boat listening, and all he heard was Zumpe talking to himself on lookout, Rethorn's footsteps in the port gangway, the wind and the parting of the water as the ship dipped her bows. He looked at his watch, set himself a time limit and kept extending the time limit. He no longer thought in detail of the actions which he had to carry out as soon as one of them – the one with the harelip or his brother – appeared beneath the boat; to begin with he had thought about them and performed each movement several times: turning around as quick as lightening in the boat, rising to his knees, thrusting out the hand that held the marlinspike, bringing it down with all the strength in his body – now he looked at his watch and thought about a final time limit.

The storm was breaking far away over the land, so that he could only see the lightning and could not hear the thunder. A warship passed with dimmed lights at high speed and cut a whitish-greenish line in the long bay. The low superstructure quickly vanished in the obscurity. An irresolute brightness lay over the islands, the first pale light of a cold daybreak. Nothing stirred on the ship.

Gombert stood up and vaulted out of the boat. He thrust the marlinspike into the pocket of his oilskin, went aft to measure the current, came back on the starboard side and walked in a crouching position past the porthole of the mess and down the gangway to the lavatory. As he stood in front of the scratched wall of the urinal he heard the swing door swing behind him, then a crunching footstep on the fluted tiles, and now a figure advanced to the next basin. Gombert recognized the profile of Dr Caspary.

'Is the storm over?' he asked.

'It doesn't look like it,' said Gombert.

'But there's nothing more to be heard.'

'It's probably gathering its strength over the shore and will come back again.'

'This would be good weather for sailing,' said Dr Caspary.

'Yes,' said Gombert.

'Would you help us? We want to get to a place near Faaborg; you can put us ashore and return to your anchorage.'

'You must discuss that with the skipper,' said Gombert.

'I'm asking you.'

'I have no say in the matter.'

'Suppose you did have a say?'

'If I had a say I should string all three of you up on the mast; and I should leave you hanging there till we made port. One of you I should deal with quite separately.'

'So,' said Dr Caspary with a smile, 'then I need have no regrets that you are not yet captain. I'm sorry, but under the circumstances I would rather refrain from giving you my good wishes for your future career.'

'In your place I should wish for something quite different,' said Gombert.

'I am already doing so,' said Dr Caspary.

They turned around at the same time, looked at one another in perplexity, as though they had only just met, and Gombert acted with the sort of instantaneous reflex only produced by complete surprise. His arm jerked up, his right fist crashed into Dr Caspary's jaw, the left followed up and smashed him full in the face, so that he fell over backwards with outspread arms, striking the back of his head a glancing blow on the edge of the basin as he went down. He fell on his back, his sunglasses broke in pieces on the tiles. His body curled up and in curling turned over on its side; Gombert knelt down beside him and listened for sounds from the gangway before slipping one arm under the back of the man's neck and lifting his face out of the shadow. One eye was closed, the other, which was watering copiously, stared at him with fixed indifference and was gradually blurred by water, and Gombert saw that it was a glass eye. He listened again, only the swing door swung irregularly to and fro, nothing stirred in the gangway. Now he grasped what had happened, and he thought over what might happen if one of them – or even if Freytag – came into the lavatory, and for an instant he thought of making off and leaving the man lying there; but perhaps, he thought, it might be the start of everything, a liberating signal which the others would act upon and which even Freytag would accept, now that it had been given and could no longer be canceled. And he lifted the body up off the tiles and got his shoulder under it so that the body doubled up and lay upon him, a dead weight.

He only needed one hand to hold Dr Caspary's body on his shoulder; he took the marlinspike in the other, pushed the swing door open with the point, left the lavatory and stepped out into the dimly lit gangway. He carried Dr Caspary past the portholes of the mess, across the deck and up onto the bridge; he opened the chartroom, let the limp body slide off his shoulder onto the chair, found an old signal line on a shelf and pulled it out, while with the other hand he held the body, which was leaning to one side and threatened to fall over. He tied Dr Caspary tightly to the chair, stepped back like a painter judging his picture, studied the fit of the bonds, stepped forward again and tied the signal line to the leg of the chair. As he straightened up he imagined he could see the trace of a smile on Dr Caspary's face, or the foretoken of a smile, so that he bent down over him and studied him attentively, with curiosity and aversion, as he might have studied a beetle that had pretended to be dead for a time and had then begun to move. And while he was standing bent over him, he heard Zumpe's voice from the door, a voice that contained suppressed delight, approval, and whispering eagerness.

'Did you catch the idiot?' he asked in a whisper from the door.

'Come in and close the bulkhead,' said Gombert.

'That's the one who is too damn clever,' said Zumpe disappointedly. 'I thought you had one of the other two.'

'He's worth just as much,' said Gombert. 'Without him they're done for.'

'I hope they realize that too,' said Zumpe.

'We'll get them one after the other,' said Gombert,

75

'neatly in turn, and I shall keep the big one for myself. Now we've made a start.'

'Does Freytag know about it?'

'Not yet. But when he does hear about it he is bound to come in with us. He can't whistle us back now.'

'Shall I fetch Rethorn?'

'No,' said Gombert. 'I'm going down to Freytag to wake him and tell him what's happened.'

'Then I'll stay here,' said Zumpe.

'Look after him,' said Gombert, 'and lock the chartroom door in case anyone comes.'

'He'll be in good hands with me,' said Zumpe, pulling out the key and putting it in his pocket. 'Go along to Freytag and tell him what he has to do.'

'Take the marlinspike,' said Gombert.

He gave Zumpe the heavy marlinspike and left the bridge, and Zumpe stationed himself with his back against the chartroom door and looked down at the deck and into the cold, hazy morning over the bay. Trailing clouds covered the horizon, the wind was growing stronger, spray flew up over the bows, splashed against the foremast and came right up to the bridge in fine drops. The big railroad ferry disappeared behind the islands.

Although he felt the desire to go into the chartroom and look at the bound man, he stayed outside to wait in front of the door for Gombert's return, but then there came a scraping, bumping noise and a sigh, which made him fear that the prisoner had fallen over with the chair, so he did open the door and go into the chartroom. Dr Caspary was still sitting on his chair; he was pulling at his bonds and thrusting his feet against the floor and trying to push and slide the chair sideways. He didn't seem to be concerned with freeing himself from his bonds, he was merely trying to move sideways, and he continued his efforts regardless of the fact that Zumpe was standing

76

in front of him. Panting, with his head back and his neck stretched, he shifted a fraction of an inch forwards.

Zumpe watched him in amazement, put the point of the marlinspike to the back of his neck and said: 'Sit still. You'll be set moving soon enough.'

'Help me,' said Dr Caspary.

'What's the matter? What do you want?'

'There is a mirror,' said Dr Caspary, jerking his head in the direction of a rectangular shaving mirror hanging at sitting height over the table.

'Leave it where it is,' said Zumpe.

'I want to look in it,' said Dr Caspary.

'You have a beautiful neck,' said Zumpe.

'Help me.'

'Your face looks fine too,' said Zumpe. 'I have always wondered what a gentleman ought to look like – now I know. If there are such things as gentlemen they must look and be like you: even when he's tied up the gentleman needs a mirror, and it would worry him terribly if he had to put an unshaven neck in the noose. Am I right?'

'Turn the chair a little to the side, or put the mirror on the table.'

'But we haven't a hairdresser on board,' said Zumpe.

'I don't need a hairdresser,' said Dr Caspary. 'I only need the mirror.'

'May I ask why?'

'In the past I often used to sit in front of the mirror and look into my face; for a time in fact it was one of my favorite occupations.'

'An occupation like that helps to pass a gentleman's time,' said Zumpe.

'I used to sit in front of my reflection with a revolver and aim at the face I saw: at this forehead, at these eyes, I aimed at the chin or between the lips; I could sit like that for hours, watching the face under the revolver.'

'You can have the mirror,' said Zumpe.

'That's all I need,' said Dr Caspary.

Zumpe took the mirror off the hook, put it on the table, and made sure that Dr Caspary could see his face in it, then he said, 'The revolver will follow in due course,' went out and locked the chartroom door.

Gombert still hadn't come back, although Zumpe had imagined that he must now be hearing his footsteps. He listened by the companion ladder, stepped into the wing of the bridge and observed the deck, and after a while he heard the footsteps of two men and thought that Gombert was coming up to the bridge with Freytag. He went over to the companion ladder to wait for them. The footsteps approached along the port gangway, stopped, were audible again, and then he saw the two brothers down at the bottom of the companion ladder – Eddie in front, on edge, suspicious, the submachine gun drawn in to his hip; behind him Eugen, weary, a cigarette dangling over his chin – saw them stop, listen behind them, and, before Zumpe could get out of sight, raise their heads both at the same time and stare at him without moving. They stared at him neither amazed nor surprised nor bewildered, but as if they expected something particular from him, a shout or a movement, perhaps even a split-second action, and probably they would have gone past down below if he had met their expectant gaze without flinching and done nothing; but Zumpe suddenly withdrew the upper part of his body and stepped back into the wing of the bridge, and immediately afterwards he heard them coming up. He took a firm grip on the marlinspike, looked at the opening of the companion ladder, and there they were on the platform of the bridge: the barrel of the submachine gun swaying in a small arc, first Eddie and then his brother.

They began to search the bridge, they walked past Zumpe to the other wing, whispered, pointed down at

78

the boat in the davits; came back without taking their eyes off him, and now came towards him.

'Where is our man?' asked Eddie.

'In the messroom,' said Zumpe. 'He has taken lodgings there.'

'He must be here,' said Eddie.

'No one has any business on the bridge,' said Zumpe.

'Don't worry,' said the giant, 'we shan't do your bridge any harm; we've wiped our feet.'

'Tell us where he is,' repeated Eddie.

'You generally know everything,' said Zumpe, 'how come you don't know that?'

'Here's a door,' said the giant and moved the latch and tried to open the door of the chartroom.

'Take your flippers off that,' said Zumpe. 'No one is allowed into the chartroom except the captain and the mate.'

Eugen shook his head, laughed an impetuous, stupid laugh and shook the door again, so that Zumpe involuntarily stepped closer, the marlinspike held ready in his pocket.

'Open up, you,' said Eugen. 'And make it snappy or there'll be trouble.'

'Take your flippers off the latch,' said Zumpe warningly.

'Come on, you dwarf, open up,' said Eddie.

'Only the captain has the right to do that, and the mate.'

'And us,' said Eddie. 'What we tell you is worth just as much as what the captain says. You don't seem to have cottoned on to that yet.'

'He's very slow on the uptake,' said Eugen. 'Too slow for a little man like that.'

The giant shook the door again, bent down to the keyhole, while Eddie watched his face as though he hoped to read there immediately what his brother discovered in the chartroom, and in this second Zumpe drew the marlinspike from his pocket and struck out. He already had his eye on the spot – a spot between Eddie's shoulder and neck – which the point of the marlinspike was to strike; but before his hand came down, Eugen, who had at once seen the bound man in the chartroom, turned his head, saw the raised hand above his brother's shoulder and gave him a quick jab with his elbow, so that Eddie stumbled back against the rail of the bridge, caught himself with his back and thrust himself off again like a boxer off the ropes, and in the movement fired.

The barrel of the submachine gun was pointing upwards at an angle with little jagged flames at its muzzle; the bullets plowed into Zumpe's body from the hip to the collarbone, flung him back into the wing of the bridge like a violent gust of wind, and he looked astonished as he dropped to his knees, knelt for a moment in amazement and then fell on his face. His feet scraped slightly on the platform of the bridge, his horn-hard, clawlike fingers felt about on either side.

'You see,' said Eugen sadly, 'you see.'

Eddie pushed the ejected cartridge cases aside with his foot and said: 'Quick, they'll be here in a moment. We must do something.'

'The doctor is in here,' said Eugen.

'Then open the door.'

'I've tried,' said Eugen, 'but the door is stronger.'

'Come away,' said Eddie. 'Stand back.'

He held the barrel of the submachine gun at an angle to the lock of the door and fired; the board splintered, ricocheting bullets whistled across the deck. Then smoke rose from the point of impact. He fired several bursts at the lock, and the bullets blew it apart and threw the door open. While Eddie swung the barrel around to the companion ladder Eugen went into the chartroom and untied Dr Caspary, who massaged his wrists and the back of his neck with a smirk, then took a cigarette from his case, carefully screwed it into his holder and lit it.

'Thanks, Eugen,' he said politely. 'I shan't forget what you have done.'

'Was it bad?' Eugen asked with concern.

'Only disappointing,' said Dr Caspary. 'They have no ideas; in everything they show and do they are hidebound, frightfully hidebound: in their imagination and in their wrongdoing.'

'We ought to beat it,' said the giant.

'Why? Now we can breakfast in peace.'

'There's a man lying out there looking down,' said Eugen. 'The dwarf, that's the way he wanted it.'

'I heard what happened,' said Dr Caspary.

'Come out of there,' shouted Eddie from the bridge.

'Eddie will get angry in a moment,' said Eugen.

'Then we had better go out,' said Dr Caspary.

Voices of the crew on deck as they left the chartroom: Freytag's voice, Rethorn's husky voice, and the cook's dismayed cries – 'There was shooting, someone fired a gun' – and then footsteps down below and a stamping on the companion ladder, till Freytag's face came up over the platform. Freytag paused when he caught sight of Eddie and the barrel of the submachine gun that was aimed at him, but he didn't duck down, he went on slowly raising himself, doggedly, with an effort, as though the muzzle he was looking into demanded all his strength; came up till the top of the companion ladder cut across his torso, stopped, hesitated, now looked at the man standing there with his legs apart, who observed him with complete and unpredictable calm and then said in a low voice:

'No further.'

Freytag obeyed. The warning gave him a feeling of security, he felt that he had reached the boundary and need expect no trouble so long as he did not overstep it, and he took his eyes off Eddie and looked across the bridge and into the wing where Zumpe lay – his hands pressed flat on the platform as though he had tried to catch his body as it fell.

'Go back,' ordered Eddie. 'Get out of the way, all of you, until we are down. We're coming down now.'

'Please clear the companion ladder,' said Dr Caspary.

And Freytag obeyed and slowly clambered down; there was a whispered consultation, and the footsteps of several men moved away along the port gangway, so that the three met no one as – with Eddie in front and Dr Caspary bringing up the rear – they climbed down and went into the mess, which the giant had taken the precaution of locking. Only when they had closed the door of the mess behind them did Freytag, Gombert, and Rethorn emerge from the galley, where they had waited, and climb up to the bridge.

Gombert knelt down beside Zumpe and turned him over: under his body lay the marlinspike which he himself had given him, and from the hip to the shoulder there stretched a bloody stripe like the suggestion of a scarf, which the bullets had plowed in him. His face still wore the same expression of anguished astonishment, rigid and final, carved like a mask. They took off their caps and looked down at Zumpe; then Freytag knelt down, opened Zumpe's jacket and emptied his pockets; placed a pipe on the deck, a jackknife, galvanized nails and a battered tobacco tin, and finally his wallet riddled with bullet holes. He opened the wallet, found the stained newspaper clipping under the strip of cellophane, and knew that it was Zumpe's obituary which he always circulated when new men came aboard. He put it all in his pocket and straightened up.

'Bring him down,' said Freytag to Gombert.

'Where to?'

'Take him into the sailroom.'

'Shall I get everything ready?' asked Gombert.

'Why do you ask?'

'When the bumboat comes – it could take him ashore.'

'I don't know,' said Freytag. 'First bring him down.'

Gombert lifted the dead man onto his shoulders and lugged him to the companion ladder, and Freytag pushed open the door of the chartroom, which was swinging to and fro, put everything that had belonged to Zumpe on the table and covered it with the logbook.

'What are you going to do?' asked Rethorn. 'We shall have to report his death, the Coast Guard Office will have to hear about it, and Zumpe's relatives will have to hear about it too.'

'He had no relatives,' said Freytag. 'I don't know where he hung out or what he did when we were in dock; I only know that nobody used to be waiting for him.'

'Then the Coast Guard Office will have to know,' said Rethorn.

'He didn't take care,' said Freytag. 'Zumpe didn't stick to what we agreed.'

'Just say you put all the blame on him.'

'No,' said Freytag, 'not on him, but on the man who cut their boat adrift in the fog. If Soltow had repaired their boat they would be off the ship by now, and we could send out our report and see to it that they didn't get as far as twenty miles.'

'I didn't cut the boat adrift,' sayd Rethorn.

'Then who did?' exclaimed Freytag.

'Not me, and I didn't tell anyone else to cut the boat adrift. I give you my word.'

'You know how much I value your word,' said Freytag contemptuously.

'It wasn't me,' said Rethorn.

'Leave me alone,' said Freytag. 'You're no use to me at the moment.'

He left Rethorn standing, pulled up the chair, sat down and looked at the logbook, then he picked it up and opened it. He spent a long time reading the last entries; he had made them himself but now they seemed to him to date from another age, to have been written by another man than the one he was now or imagined himself to be: state of the sea, weather reports, movements of shipping in the bay – it all seemed to him incredible, and the ever-recurring close 'no special events' seemed to him like a comfortable lie with which he had attempted to cover up his omissions or his inability to find out what had really happened; and as he felt this he spread out the logbook and began to write. In the past, ten lines had been enough to polish off a day and be done with it; now – and he only noticed it when the whole page was full – an extra sheet had to be inserted, which he put behind the dated page and fastened with a paper clip. He wrote down everything, what he had seen himself and what he had heard: he noted down his orders, the actions of the crew and the behavior of the three castaways, from the first day on. He believed that he had omitted neither his conjectures nor the crucial passages of the conversations which he quoted from memory, and after he had written four pages about the first day he had the feeling that this day was not yet completed and that there was still something missing.

Suddenly he raised his head. The door with the smashed lock was no longer banging; a foot had been thrust into the crack, a hand put around the splintered board. Freytag immediately shut the logbook, put it back on the shelf and drew the things that had been in Zumpe's pockets towards him with a sweeping movement of the arm. He felt the door open behind him, felt the nearness of the man who entered, his suppressed breathing, but he did not look around, although the alien presence was

84

trying to force him to. And then he heard the soft, clear voice of Dr Caspary.

'I had to come back again,' he said. 'I was afraid I should disturb you, but I had to tell you how much I regretted the incident.'

'It wasn't an incident,' said Freytag, 'it was murder.'

'You forget that it was done in self-defense.'

'What I saw, I saw.'

'What one man sees is not enough.'

'Go away,' said Freytag, 'go to your men.'

'My men likewise regret what happened.'

'You and your men have never regretted anything.'

'Perhaps you are right,' said Dr Caspary. 'We have probably never regretted anything, because he who regrets does not wish to forget, and we want to forget completely. In this respect my men and I are alike – as you surmise. Nevertheless I came up here at least to tell you that what happened need not have happened.'

'Is that all?' asked Freytag.

'No,' said Dr Caspary politely, 'by no means. I have something else to say to you. We have decided to leave you; unfortunately we cannot open the door and go, since it is most certainly not vouchsafed to everyone to walk on the water. We require assistance, and if your dinghy is not ready in two days you will assist us to reach our destination with your ship. We shall make certain of your assistance, Captain, be sure of that. I know your answer and your convictions – don't let things reach the point where you are forced to learn how much both are worth. There is something that is stronger than all convictions – at least in case of emergency.'

'You think yourself very strong, I know; people talk like that when they have a revolver in their pocket, but I should like to hear you if you were unarmed or if we also had arms.'

'What you have observed is not new, Captain. Just as

85

today a revolver may alter the structure of a sentence, so the first sling changed the tone of conversation between men. He who has a weapon always finds a different relationship to language than an unarmed man. And by the way, I have decided to carry a gun after all – although I hate having anything heavy in my pocket; tell that to your man who considered the lavatory a good enough place to knock me down. I only hope it happened without your knowledge.'

'Make no mistake,' said Freytag, 'make no mistake: if you try to riase the anchor of this ship by force, then you will find yourself in trouble. You can try anything you like on this ship, but not that. You'll get a surprise.'

Dr Caspary caught sight of the fountain pen on the table, glanced at the logbook on the shelf, took it out, opened it and began to read. The frame of his sunglasses had been mended with thin wire, one lens was missing, so that his face now had an owl-like look. He read what Freytag had written right through, then he put the logbook down on the table and tore out the page.

'You will permit me, won't you?' he said. 'I am only acting in accordance with my view that it would be good for your ship at least to have a secret, a dark spot. Moreover, you already know that we are not particularly interested in preserving our tracks.'

'The bumboat,' Rethorn shouted across from the look-out to the bridge.

'What does that mean?' asked Dr Caspary.

'Just what I said,' said Freytag. 'The bumboat is coming alongside.'

'Visitors then,' said Dr Caspary.

'Pleasant visitors,' said Freytag.

'Is the boat staying here long?'

'That depends on us,' said Freytag, 'and on what stories we have to tell them.'

86

'I'm afraid you won't have much of a story to tell them.'

'There is always some story to tell.'

'Very well,' said Dr Caspary, 'we shall vacate the mess and move up here on the bridge – at least for the duration of the visit. You know our position, Captain, and you know what under certain circumstances it might force us to do. Bear that in mind while you are telling your stories.'

'What are you driving at?' asked Freytag.

'That you keep silent on the vital point – as is always the case in a good story. There is no need for everything to be understood, and a few obscurities have to be accepted. If your visitors start asking questions or showing surprise, then refer them to the encyclopedia.'

'You are – '

'Yes, what were you going to say?'

'I should like to get you in my hands once,' said Freytag. 'All three of you, one after the other, or any way you like, openly, man to man, and then I'd like to have a little chat with you. You would become so small, so small.'

'Make no mistake, Captain: man is afforded a certain stature not merely by his motives, but also by his anatomy.'

Freytag put the logbook back in its place and went down to the accommodation ladder, where part of the crew were standing waiting for the bumboat, which was heading straight for them lying deep in the water. The bumboat's long projecting bow cut through the crests of the waves, thrusting the water up to the narrow fenders; rolling, it approached from aft, swung out, and then a man in the stern waved his hand, stood up, took the tiller between his thighs and in this position maneuvered the boat to the accommodation ladder.

Without turning his head, Freytag looked up at the

bridge and saw the two brothers crouching behind the railing and knew that they had their weapons in their hands. Before the line fell down to the bumboat with a slapping sound Freytag signed to Gombert, and Gombert went up to each of those standing by the accommodation ladder and whispered something to him. Then the men from the bumboat came on deck, two men in heavy jackets, tall, unshaven; they wore black peaked caps on their heads and their trousers were tucked into their boots. They said 'Morning' and put their hands in their pockets and sniffed in the direction of the mess.

'If I don't get something to drink here,' said one of them, 'I shall die of thirst on the spot. I'm simply dizzy with thirst.'

'Then let's go down to the mess,' said Freytag.

First they drank rum and tea and sat under the darkened portraits of former lightship skippers, while the others took on goods and post from the bumboat. Freytag pushed a box of very good cigars across to them, took out a bottle of very good cognac, and they knocked out their pipes and left the cups of rum and tea standing and one of them said:

'Generally all you get at a sale is rubbish; with you it's the other way around: you put out the best stuff at the end-of-the-year sale.'

'What does it feel like to be on your last watch?' asked the other.

'Different from usual,' said Freytag. 'I can't imagine that we are leaving yere.'

'That's what I thought,' said the first one.

'Do you know Bohnsack?' asked the other. 'His ship used to lie out in front of the channel, and when they towed it in he bought the superstructure of an old steamer that was going to be broken up, had it taken ashore and arranged everything as it had been on his ship. It's exactly

88

like on board ship. Will you fix up something like that for yourself too?'

'I don't know,' said Freytag. 'We're not on land yet.'

'But it won't be long now.'

'I should be glad if I had it all behind me.'

'Why aren't you drinking?' asked the first man. 'It's very good cognac, besides which it's yours.'

'Not now,' said Freytag.

'Then here's to you,' said the second man.

They drank, sighed, then the first man said: 'We ought to say good-bye to the old tub before she's towed in.'

'That's not necessary,' said Freytag.

'Just a tour of inspection,' said the second man.

'Have another drink,' said Freytag.

'A good idea,' said the first man, drawing on his cigar with closed eyes.

'I've brought you something,' said the second man, 'a farewell present.'

He carefully lifted a cardboard box onto the table, undid the string and invited Freytag to raise the lid.

'A cake?' asked Freytag.

'Like last time,' said the first man, 'only this time with cherries. I'd eat it in a hurry, because during your last three days a lot of people will come alongside, and you'll be able to open a pastry shop, they'll bring so many cakes aboard.'

'I'll find Trittel and tell him to make us some coffee,' said Freytag.

'Leave it to me,' said the second man, 'I'll look around a bit at the same time.'

'I'll find him quicker,' said Freytag. 'I'll be back in a moment. Meanwhile help yourselves to another cognac.'

'Don't mind if I do,' said the first man.

'It's as cozy as at home on your ship,' said the second man. 'So I won't disturb the coziness.'

'There's a shell lying here,' said the first man. 'Small shot. Do you shoot ducks?'

Freytag took the shell out of his hand. 'Fred dropped it,' he said. 'My boy. I've got him on board with me.'

'Hurry up,' said the second man, 'otherwise we shall empty the bottle.'

'I don't know which to admire most,' Dr Caspary said to Freytag, 'your prudence or your steadiness. Anyhow, your friends would scarcely have been able to get into the boat without your help, whereas you yourself look as though you had been resting all the time. Do you think the bumboat will find its way back safely?'

'That's not your worry,' said Freytag.

'But they are your friends,' said Dr Caspary, 'and they were listening badly when they left. If it were up to me I should be worrying about them.'

Freytag was sitting in a canvas-covered deck chair, gazing after the vaguely winking stern light of the bumboat as it vanished into the pallid afternoon darkness. They had drunk two lots of coffee together and cognac before the coffee and with the coffee, and the two tall men in the heavy jackets would have forgotten that they had to go back if Freytag had not reminded them. For years they had been chugging out to the lightship, but they had never got so gloriously drunk as this time; in the end neither of them had spoken any more, they had sat facing each other in silence, with drooping eyelids, from time to time straightening up their bodies with a jerk as they threatened to slump forward, which brought them around, then they clicked their tongues, and, as if this were a word of command, grasped their glasses. Under the arm which one man had rested on the table Freytag had kept the mess door under observation, and had looked past his red ears out of the porthole, and when the wind died down, pale darkness fell over the bay and Freytag knew that trouble was to be expected, he stood up and took the men to their boat and went up to the bridge. The whistling in the aerial wires had ceased, the ship lay motionless on a long anchor chain. Two porpoises darted by, leapt into the air, dived in with bodies bent, rose to the surface again with little hissing fountains; they swam out to the open sea, cutting a track across the lusterless water. The sea was now without reflected light, dull and gray; the dark blue of the line of islands had vanished, the warning green of the wreck-buoy, nowhere was there the stabbing, coppery flash of turbulent water, and the coast, which had lain like a shimmering reflection across the horizon – steel-gray and as if floating above the water – sank with the pallid darkness and disappeared from sight. They sent out storm warnings.

Dr Caspary put the narrow strap of the binoculars around his neck; he brought out a chair from the chart-room, made a gesture in Freytag's direction that was a request for his permission, and sat down. For a long while he observed the bumboat through the glasses, saw the hazy light sinking lower over the sea till finally it seemed to be gliding over the water as if from nowhere, murky, flickering uncertainly, and then suddenly tipped over into the sea and vanished.

'I guess they'll soon be ashore now,' said Dr Caspary. 'Anyhow they will be home before the storm breaks. You do think we must expect trouble, don't you, Captain?'

'You must expect plenty of trouble,' said Freytag.

'It finds me not unprepared,' said Dr Caspary. 'I'm always expecting trouble; for many years I have reckoned with a whole bundle of demand notes every day.'

'You'll get them,' said Freytag, 'perhaps very soon.'

'So much the better,' said Dr Caspary. 'After all, a

debtor reckons with occasionally seeing a bill of exchange; if he always fails to appear on the due date people start getting suspicious and wondering what's behind it.'

'You won't be forgotten,' said Freytag.

'I'm not so sanguine,' said Dr Caspary.

Up to now Freytag had spoken out over the railing, without looking at Dr Caspary; now he turned around and said:

'In my life I have met men whom I found repulsive the moment I set eyes on them – types I would have liked to tow behind the ship like a log and to have dragged through all the waters of the earth, but none of them were as repulsive to me as you. I sometimes wonder whether a thing like you can ever have had a father.'

'You'll laugh,' said Dr Caspary, 'I had one; and since you have inquired about him I'll tell you. He was a well-known, pious man, well known at least to people who traveled by railroad. Since you yourself haven't used the railroad much you're not likely to know him, but a lot of people would remember at once when I mentioned my father's name. Not long after the First World War my father had kiosks put up in almost all the stations in North Germany, in which he sold southern fruit and religious tracts; on the kiosks there stood in large letters REFRESHMENTS FOR EVERY JOURNEY and underneath, slightly smaller, TRUST IN REINHOLD CASPARY. This was also on the fruit bags, while the religious tracts had titles referring to the condition of the traveler. Things like ALL ROADS LEAD TO YOU, or THE JOURNEY THROUGH THE EYE OF A NEEDLE, and once I read the title HE ALONE BRINGS YOU SO SWEETLY TO YOUR DESTINATION – which might very well be taken to mean my father and his blood oranges. The kiosks did well; my father had realized that people on trains suffer more from thirst than from hunger and to this modest discovery he owed his fortune.'

Dr Caspary stopped and smiled, lit a cigarette and went on: 'You are the first man, Captain, to whom I have told this; in fact it is the first time I have ever spoken of my father. I didn't think much of him.'

Freytag looked around in surprise. As once before, the remark carried conviction and sounded like a confession, and he had the feeling that Dr Caspary wasn't only trying to entertain him. He said – and the moment he said it he realized that it wasn't what he had meant to say: 'Your father must have thought just as much of you.'

'Quite right,' said Caspary. 'He indicated that often enough, and soon after my father had made a fortune he rented out the kiosks, buried himself in his room, and showed an interest in only two things: the Bible and our family history. As far as the Holy Scriptures are concerned, he became a well-known Biblical exegete whose commentaries on the Old Testament prophets were in great demand for the Sunday papers, although, as my father gave people to understand, they did not pay well for them. As regards our family history, my father discovered to his concern that it did not go back as far as the Crusades, and worse still, as he hunted through the records he found something that intensified his concern still more: every forty years – he discovered and announced this publicly on my sixteenth birthday – there emerges from our not very remarkable family a remarkable black sheep, an habitual thief, a swindler, a murderer, to which he added, however, that they were without exception gifted black sheep. He summed up the conclusion at which he had arrived in the words, "Now forty clean years have passed," and as he said this he could think of nothing else to do but to look intently and with an unspoken question at me, although he might just as well have looked at my twin brother Ralph. Anyhow, that evening I did the following: I looked at myself in the mirror and saw a stranger.'

A violent gust of wind roared across the ship and the water, which began to ripple like corrugated iron; the sea was churned up and, while wide areas of the bay were still smooth and lusterless as though protected by an invisible fence, elsewhere it ran in ruffled folds towards the shore. The ship seemed to rise as the gust struck it, reeled slightly and swung around, and the bowsprit turned slowly, as though trying to bring itself into the direction from which a fresh gust might come. A rattling noise rose into the ship from the chain locker in the bows. Gombert cleared the forecastle and went forward and looked down at the chain, which was sagging down to the bottom. A coastal schooner was casting anchor beyond the islands.

'Now it seems to be starting,' murmured Dr Caspary indifferently.

Freytag said nothing and turned up the collar of his jacket.

'Anyhow,' said Dr Caspary, 'you can imagine how I felt when my father looked at me so intently. It almost appeared as if he considered me called or chosen to play the part of the black sheep demanded by the family tradition. I can't say that I was dismayed by this; I simply began to turn the idea over in my mind – without starting to torture flies in my room – and when my brother subsequently decided to study law I decided to do the same. We sat through the same lectures, wrote the same essays, and everybody – with the exception of my father, since he died while we were at the university – already foresaw that our joint efforts would lead to a lawyer's office with the letter heading CASPARY & CASPARY.

'These people were almost right, but then – and in this connection I think of the Old Testament prophets upon whom my father so much enjoyed writing commentaries

– our family tradition claimed its dues. I must say that on the first occasion I acted instinctively or spontaneously. I happened to have witnessed an act of blackmail; I was indignant with the blackmailer and could see no other way of punishing him than to blackmail him in his turn myself. His compliance with my demands seemed to me proof that my action was justified, but at the same time I felt a wider, more general justification for future activities in this field. This wider justification was afforded by the fact that exactly forty "clean" years had passed in the history of my family and that a black sheep was due, a fact which led me to suppose that my family would make all the allowances to which an inglorious exception is entitled: special sufferings, special vices, and a special morality.

'Since one can also err in the choice of one's crimes, I took my time and planned with circumspection. In order to bring off something remarkable one must be independent – a condition of universal application that obtained in my case thanks to my father, who, for all I know, might one day have himself persuaded me to see to it that the law of the family was fulfilled. . . . Are you still listening to me? Good . . . . So I began to observe my inclinations and my needs, and I soon ascertained that I suffered from a marked hunger for life; I wanted to experience everything it is possible for a man to experience; I wanted to absorb, collect, and seize upon more than can be acquired in one life, in one existence. We are all vassals of ourself, caught like the insect in amber, we are crucified on this one life, and every alien experience has first to be smuggled past the fortified gateways of our ego. This didn't suit me; I didn't want to be only myself, to live only in this miserable identity as Wolfram Caspary, and so I began systematically to provide myself with several lives . . . . Does this still interest you? . . .'

Dr Caspary paused, rubbed the chunky signet ring on

his hip, thoughtfully, as though to wipe away a dust layer of memory, then he laid one hand on Freytag's shoulder and pointed with the other at an object drifting in the darkness.

'There,' he said, 'do you see that?'

It was a dully shimmering object that was being driven past by the choppy, turbulent sea, and Freytag rose and gazed after it without saying a word. The bow now plunged deep and shipped breakers whose water poured frothing over the middle deck, and the ship tugged hard at the anchor chain and seemed to rear up against its bonds. The wind whistled in the aerial wires and the shrouds, lights flared up on the islands and blinked uncertainly. The sea was covered with white horses.

He's crazy, thought Freytag, *he is one of those who have been dropped on their head. He's just one of those fellows for whom life isn't enough, because they don't manage to make a success of one single thing.*

'Listen,' said Dr Caspary – and he raised his voice to make himself better understood – 'this was how I found a starting point for what I planned: I provided myself with three lives. One more or less fell into my lap, or it was brought to me like a dish which I hadn't ordered but which looked so good that I nevertheless decided to eat it: the life of my twin brother Ralph. I assumed it after we had capsized with our sailboat in the Elbe estuary. Since I was uncertain how much I could trust in my abilities as a swimmer – you know that drowning people are inclined to cling – I dared not waste my little strength on attempts at life-saving that would probably have proved fruitless. With a great effort I succeeded in swimming ashore, my brother drowned. I took over his legal practice, had myself declared dead, and acquired a life as a Hamburg lawyer . . . . Are you listening? I haven't finished yet . . .'

Freytag had risen to his feet now went into the chart-room and fastened the door, which had been banging to and fro. He stayed for a while in the chartroom, then he came out and looked over the vessel, which was shipping a great deal of water, shook itself after every impact of the sea and straightened up as though after a blow. The cold cigarette between his lips was wet with spray, and he tasted the bitter tobacco juice. Like a glaring arrow the light from their beacon flashed into the low-hanging darkness, went out and flared up again. Out on the open sea flashlight signals were being exchanged.

'That was the first lie with which I provided myself,' said Dr Caspary.

'That's enough,' said Freytag, eyeing the man with a look of attentive contempt.

'Now comes the second.'

'You will tell that later to your judge,' said Freytag. 'I haven't got time.'

'Doesn't my life interest you?' asked Dr Caspary.

'More than may be convenient for you,' said Freytag. 'But I have no time now. I have to see to the ship. We're going to have a storm during the night.'

'May I stay up here?'

'Do what you like?'

'One more thing, Captain. Your mate didn't cut the boat loose. It was I; I cut the rope and pushed the boat out into the fog.'

Freytag, who was already on the companion ladder, turned around and came back.

'Why did you do that?' he asked.

'Oh,' said Dr Caspary, 'I wanted to prevent a second shipwreck; I wanted to avoid sailing a mile out and then getting stuck. A good mechanic can fix it like that. I wanted to travel quite safely, Captain, and I think there is no better guarantee of reaching our destination than if we sail with you, with the lightship. That's why I cut

98

loose our boat. It looked to me too much like a trap – and so does your dinghy. Can you understand that?'

Freytag realized what Dr Caspary was banking on at this moment; he saw him involuntarily duck, put one hand in his pocket and feel something in his pocket and quietly hold it.

'Well?' he asked. 'When can I tell you the rest of my story, Captain? I should like to tell you the rest of it. I have never before met a man in whom I have confided like this, Captain. What can that be due to? To the completeness with which we understand one another? To your and our situation? Or do I want to tell you all about myself because we each hold the other in the palm of our hand? Every man resembles his adversary, he has no more intimate relationship to anyone.'

Freytag didn't answer. He turned around and climbed down the companion ladder, and he knew that Dr Caspary was standing above him and smiling down upon him. He went into his cabin, put on sea boots, his rubber raincoat and a woolen cap; then he stood and listened, listened to the creaking of the timbers, to the creaking sounds in the ship's side, while he held tight to the tubular iron bars of his bunk. *So he caught on*, thought Freytag, *he realized what I meant to do, because Soltow can't have told him, and Soltow is the only one who knew. He saw through everything: that we only wanted to push them out a mile into the bay, where they would have been a sitting target for the police. So that plan is scotched and he will try to force us – yes, he and the others will force us to go to the forecastle, and they will stand there with their guns and revolvers, all three of them, and the barrels of their weapons will point this way and that and show us what to do. They will try it, they have no other chance of getting away. Now we must be prepared for it.*

The ship dropped away under him and rose as though trying to stand vertical on its bowsprit. He was flung

99

against the rails of the bunk, cushioned himself against the shock by swiftly stretching out his hands in front of him, and heard the chairs slide across the floor and crash into the wall. When the ship fell back into the water there was a dull thud and a shudder ran through the hull. Again the ship dropped away and heeled over heavily; the locker door flew open, Fred's case slipped off the top shelf and bumped across the cabin. *Perhaps it's time* thought Freytag, *the time of the storm may bring a change. Now we must try something new.* He considered going up to Philippi and talking to him, although he knew what would happen as soon as the Coast Guard Office had learned of their situation: they would send a police launch and instruct him and the crew to cooperate with the police, and the Coast Guard Office would be in no doubt that this was the best advice they could give. But it was easy enough to foresee what would happen on board as soon as the police launch appeared. He thought of Gombert and what he had tried to start when he put Dr Caspary in the chartroom; at that time Freytag was against it, because he had his own plan, but now that his own plan could no longer be put into operation would he still try to upset what Gombert – or any other member of the crew – might do because he found it necessary to make a start? Freytag thought about it without making up his mind. He put the case and the chairs on the bunk, went down the gangway with bent elbows and on into the bows and down into the sailroom. The ship was rolling heavily. He dropped down on all fours, crawled to the sailroom and now heard the water crashing against the bows, he heard it so clearly and felt it so close that he involuntarily drew in his head. He hastily grasped the latch and pushed open the door to the sailroom; his hand felt up the wall to where the light switch must be; he turned the switch, the light did not come on. Feeling his way with his hands held out in front of him, he crawled into the sailroom, squatted down with his back against the wall and turned the electric light switch again. The room remained dark and he simply squatted there and thought of Zumpe, who was lying in front of him or beside him in the clammy darkness among the emergency sails. Would Caspary force them to use the emergency sails?

For an instant he was sure he heard footsteps, a curse and the bumping of a body in the gangway, and he thought he heard Fred's voice and waited, but no one came forward to the sailroom. He left the sailroom, crawled back on all fours and climbed up to the chartroom. It was empty. He went onto the bridge, and here too he met no one – although he had counted on meeting Dr Caspary – and as he was about to go across to the lookout Eddie stood in his path. Freytag recognized him at once: Eddie was holding onto the iron railing with one hand, in the other he held the submachine gun, the barrel of which he pressed with an effort into Freytag's hip. Freytag smiled as a wave lifted the ship and dashed it down again, so that Eddie crashed against the railing, groaned, and whipped the gun back into position once more.

'What's the matter?' yelled Freytag.

'My brother is gone,' yelled Eddie.

'I haven't seen him!'

'He's gone!'

Eddie beckoned, they went out of the wind, held tight to each other, and brought their faces close together – so close that they imagined they could feel the warmth of one another's breath.

'Where is he?' shouted Eddie.

'I've no time to look after him,' said Freytag.

Eddie made a furious movement.

'I shall find him,' he cried threateningly.

'Perhaps he has lost his way,' shouted Freytag. 'You so seldom come out of the messroom.'

'I shall make up for that,' shouted Eddie and turned away and stumbled off into the darkness. Freytag stayed out of the wind, looked out across the stern: the clouds were flying so low across the bay that the flashing beacon light caught them; the sea was alight with whitecaps that reared up and scattered glittering. There was rain in the air, the wind was not increasing. *He is prudent and armed*, thought Freytag. *No one will try on him what Gombert tried on Caspary. He's probably lying in the latrine vomiting.* He decided to go down to the lavatory and after that to look for Fred. Puddles had gathered in the hollows of the iron platform and spray lashed his face like hail as he stepped out into the wind again and wondered about the safest way to get to the companion ladder. He looked at the platform, saw that the ventilation hatch of the galley was open, and imagined he could smell the aroma of very good coffee. A dim shimmer of light lay on the slanting hatch. Freytag bent down with his back pressed against the bench with the life jackets, the flying spray swept over him, the warmth rested on his face like an open hand. At the long scrubbed table down below in the galley Trittel and Eugen sat drinking coffee; they were sitting facing each other at one corner of the table, Trittel was still wearing his cook's cap, which threw a long, threatening shadow that moved over the deck and over the wall when the cook rose and fetched fresh coffee from the stove. His lined face, his lean neck and lean arms, were a greenish color in the uncertain light. When the pots and lids began to tinkle in their racks he raised his face and looked at them mutely, as though to warn them. He never looked at the man with the harelip. Eugen was resting the upper part of his body on the table, holding the steaming coffee in

102

front of his face and drinking in sharp little sips. Out of his pocket projected the butt of a large-caliber revolver.

Freytag watched them, listened and waited for one of them to say something, but he heard nothing, saw only Eugen's grinning face and Trittel's greenish face with the eyeless orbits in deep shadow, and he drew himself up again, crossed the platform to the companion ladder, went down to the lavatory and finally back into his cabin.

Fred lay fully dressed on the bunk. He didn't move, didn't raise his head as his father came in, he just lay there, his feet spread out under the bar of the bunk to keep from being thrown out.

Freytag went up to the boy's bunk, looked down at him and said: 'Fred.'

The boy sat up without a word, pulled his sweater down over his belt, jumped out of the bunk.

'Where are you going?' asked Freytag.

'Outside,' said Fred tonelessly.

'This is no weather for you to be out in,' said Freytag. 'I should lie down and sleep.'

'I can do that at home,' said Fred.

'Perhaps I should have left you there.'

'Why?' said Fred. 'I find it very interesting here. You couldn't have offered me anything better. I've learned a lot here.'

'Take care what you say, you're getting careless,' said Freytag.

'Let me pass,' said Fred.

Freytag squeezed back against the door of the locker and let Fred pass; the boy stood irresolutely in the gangway, looked back, then made off in the direction of Philippi's and Rethorn's cabins.

Why am I here? thought Freytag. *Why did I look for him, why am I running around looking for one of them? Has it reached a point where they're all against me? Why*

*am I not on the bridge? I knew how he would answer me
– so why?*

A long, flapping shadow appeared on the wall that
struck him as familiar, and before Freytag turned around
he knew that it was the shadow of Trittel's cook's cap
that topped his lined face like a flour-white Chinese
lantern, crumpled and slightly sagging.

'Come,' said Freytag, 'come on in,' and he turned
around and saw Trittel as he had never seen him before.
The cook stood in the doorway panting, his mouth wide
open, his eyes staring with silent horror; his Adam's
apple went down his throat as he gulped, his hands
moved violently under his apron, drew together, clasped,
while his lean body swayed. He remained standing by
the door as though not daring to enter Freytag's cabin.

'Come in,' ordered Freytag and shut the door behind
the cook. Trittel obeyed, walked over to the bunk with
dragging, uncertain steps and an expression of stricken
servility.

'Sit down,' ordered Freytag.

'It has happened,' said the cook. He rubbed his hands
together under his apron, stood in front of Freytag and
suddenly fell on his knees before him. 'You must help
me,' he said with his head thrown back, 'now it has
happened.'

'What?'

'It happened all of a sudden, I don't know how it came
about.'

'Tell me what has happened,' ordered Freytag.

'I can still feel it in my hand,' said the cook, 'the way
he threw himself up onto the knife.'

'You were drinking coffee together.'

'Did you see it?' asked Trittel in dismay.

'No,' said Freytag, 'I only saw you drinking coffee
together.'

'He came in and asked for coffee,' said the cook in a

104

low voice. 'I had some hot coffee and I gave him some and we drank together.'

'Get up,' said Freytag. 'Come, sit down on the bunk.'

'To begin with, he said nothing, and then he started talking about Zumpe and asked if we had put him on ice or what we were going to do with him.'

'Is he up there in the galley?' asked Freytag.

Trittel shook his head. 'He drank his coffee and didn't take his eyes off me, and after he had drunk his coffee he wanted something to eat. I gave him some bread and sardines, and he ate, and while he was eating I was able to walk to and fro without him watching me, and all at once I thought of all you and I thought you would expect it of me and that you would do the same thing in my place. You would have done it, wouldn't you?'

'What happened?' asked Freytag.

'I had just been shaving – I know you don't like me to shave in the galley – and I saw the razor lying there and was going to pick it up, but I didn't do so. I took the kitchen knife. As I struck him – I can still feel it in my hand – he was about to jump up, but he never got up and he fell down by the stool. You would have done the same, wouldn't you? My God, tell me what you would have done?'

'Where is he now?' asked Freytag.

'He's no longer on board,' said Trittel. 'I was carrying him out when a wave swept him overboard. Now there are only two of them in the mess.'

'Yes,' said Freytag, 'now there are only two of them.'

'You must help me,' said the cook. 'You will help me, won't you? I did it for you and for the others and for Zumpe. Say something!'

'It has happened,' said Freytag.

'Shouldn't I have done it?'

'We'll find out,' said Freytag. 'Soon.'

No storm blew up overnight. When the rain started, cold and teeming like a cloudburst, the wind abated; the sea became calmer, and towards morning the coastal schooner moored under the islands weighed anchor. Only the darkness remained, a low darkness, and high above the ship a mighty draft blew through the air. Freytag was asleep on the chair in the chartroom when Gombert spotted the mine, rushed in and shook him awake and gave him the glasses. At first he simply couldn't see it, although he only examined the sector Gombert indicated; but then he saw the black cap with the horns poking up slightly out of the water, saw the lethargic, clumsy rocking of the black mass with the water swishing over it, and all of a sudden the mine went under without leaving a trace. The bow of the lightship was pointing towards the open sea and the mine was drifting towards it, rocking, with agonizing slowness, like the bulky body of a dead beast carried off by the sea. Every time it dived out of sight Freytag had difficulty in finding it again: at times it rose so high that the black curve was discernible; at times only the splashing of the water betrayed where the mine was. Occasionally it remained out of sight for so long that Freytag thought it had sunk and wouldn't rise again, and then the lead caps unexpectedly thrust up their horns out of a wave.

Gombert stood beside him impatiently while he observed the mine.

'Can you see it?' he kept asking, and Freytag said:

'Yes, I can see it.'

'It's drifting towards us,' said Gombert.

'I can see it,' said Freytag.

He lowered the glasses, the mine was six hundred yards from the ship and drifting very slowly towards them.

'Do you think it's going to hit us?' asked Gombert.

'It looks like it,' said Freytag.

'Perhaps it's no longer live. Maybe it has been in the water so long that it has been put out of action.'

'We can wait and see,' said Freytag. 'If it explodes, it was in working order.'

'I thought they had cleared them all away from here and that the water outside the bay was free from mines.'

'It is free from mines – apart from a few they didn't find.'

'What shall we do?'

'We must persuade it to make a detour around the ship or to sink before it reaches us.'

He returned the glasses to Gombert, ran his fingers over his face, fetched the half cigarette from the chartroom and left the bridge. Freytag went down to the mess. He hadn't seen Dr Caspary since learning from Trittel what had happened during the night in the galley, nor had he seen Eddie again. He banged twice with his fist on the door, there was a scraping sound of the legs of chairs dragging across the floor, then Dr Caspary opened the door and stood in the crack. He gave a surprised smile and said:

'I'm sorry, but I can't let you in now; one of my friends isn't ready. Is there anything I can do for you?'

'I must speak to you,' said Freytag.

'What about? I thought everything was clear between us?'

'Would you come out on deck? I don't want to disturb your two friends.'

'They are healthy and need a lot of sleep.'

'I hope they don't both sleep at the same time,' said Freytag.

'At the proper moment they will both be awake,' said Dr Caspary.

Freytag noticed that he was lying and also felt that Dr Caspary was trying to conceal something: an insecurity, a certain disappointment, and at this moment Freytag knew that the man standing facing him in spotted sunglasses was lying out of fear.

'The ship is in danger,' said Freytag in a low voice.

'I know,' said Dr Caspary, 'but we are always in danger. We ought to have got used to it by now. Anything else?'

'We need your help,' said Freytag.

'For that I must comb my hair,' said Dr Caspary. 'Just a moment, wait for me.'

He went back into the mess, returned after a short time and bared his forearms by stretching out his hands and making his jacket sleeves ride up – as a sign that he was ready to help.

'Come with me,' said Freytag.

They climbed up to the lookout platform, Freytag took the glasses from Gombert and handed them to Dr Caspary; then he pointed in the direction from which the mine was drifting, and said:

'Look through the glasses. You will see what I mean. Look carefully: a mine is drifting towards us, about five hundred yards from the ship.'

Dr Caspary took a step to one side before putting the glasses to his eyes and studying the sea.

'Yes,' he said, 'I can see it – now it has gone again.'

'It's drifting towards the ship,' said Freytag.

'How can I help you?' asked Dr Caspary. 'Shall I persuade the mine to drift in a different direction? Or shall I defuse it with words?'

'This concerns you just as much as it does us,' said Freytag.

'Very good,' said Dr Caspary. 'So there is something before which we are equal; all at once a situation may arise which makes us forget the condition existing on board. Suddenly we are all prisoners in a situation in which we are dependent upon one another.'

'It is drifting slowly,' said Freytag. 'We still have time.'

'Perhaps it isn't live,' said Gombert.

'There are mines that have lain in the water for twenty years, and for twenty years ships have sailed over them, and when they have been forgotten they one day blow up.'

'How can I help you then?' asked Dr Caspary.

'We must blow it up by shooting at it,' said Freytag, 'before it comes too near the ship. If you or your friends won't do it, then I shall.'

'You see, Captain, that's the advantage of being armed: if one day a mine floats towards you, you can keep the thing at a comfortable distance.'

'Will you help us?' asked Freytag.

'I shall talk to my friends,' said Dr Caspary, 'and if they agree we shall do something.'

He went off down to the mess, smiling, and Gombert looked at Freytag from the side and said: 'I wouldn't have done that in your place.'

'What would you have done then?'

'I don't know,' said Gombert, 'but not that. I shouldn't have let myself be helped by them.'

'You can sometimes get into a scrape,' said Freytag, 'which only your adversary can get you out of. I personally should never accept their help, but the ship needs it and the ship is more important than anything else.'

'Have you forgotten Zumpe?'

'I have forgotten nothing.'

'Who will explode the mine,' asked Gombert, 'the idiot or his brother?'

'His brother,' said Freytag, 'and it will be the last time he fires his gun. I can't tell you more than that.'

'Has something happened?'

'Yes, something has happened, and you will hear about it soon enough.'

Now Eddie and Dr Caspary came up on deck, and they beckoned to them. Eddie brushed aside the binoculars

Freytag offered him; he observed the sea with his naked eye from a point several paces away from the men; all nonchalance had vanished from his movements, his face wore an expression of weary brutality. He glanced fleetingly in the direction from which the mine was drifting, he couldn't find it, and when Dr Caspary showed it to him he signed to the men to step even farther back; then he laid the submachine gun on the rail, took aim and waited.

Nobody looked at him any more; they all stood in silence and watched with anguished anticipation the spot on the water at which the black horns must appear. When they appeared Eddie fired, and the bullets hissed across the water; a chain of fountains was thrown up, fifty or even a hundred yards in front of the mine, which swayed away under the impact of the bullets like a body taking cover. Eddie kicked the empty cartridge cases overboard, put the submachine gun to his shoulder and waited, and now the mine was thrown up so that the round black outline of its top was clearly visible above the water. Eddie fired two bursts, raising the gun as he did so, and they could clearly hear the bullets striking the metal body and they saw the fountains spurting up around the mine.

'Very good,' cried Dr Caspary, 'you've hit it, Eddie.'

'The damn thing won't explode,' said Eddie.

'You must hit the horns,' said Gombert.

'Bright boy,' said Eddie. 'My granny would have told me that too.'

The spot at which the mine now rolled and drifted lethargically was marked by splashing water; it had to be just under the surface, and this time Eddie didn't wait till it emerged but took aim and fired, lowered the gun and fired again. Thereupon the sea gathered together as though in a mighty grip, broke away, rose quivering as if a mountain were rising from the water; a fountain of spray and foam shot up, seemed for a moment to stand still, and then darted up again, as though impelled by a fresh force. A shudder ran across the sea, a pressure wave followed it, and the tons of water thrown up by the explosion fell back with a mighty splash.

Eddie stared incredulously at the phenomenon he himself had induced, and Dr Caspary rubbed his signet ring on his hip with quick, jerky movements and said:

'Very good, Eddie. That was the best thing I have ever seen you do.'

'So it was live,' said Freytag to Gombert. 'It was still in working order.'

'I would never have believed it,' said Gombert.

'Is that what you wanted?' asked Eddie as he drew the submachine gun to his hip, walked away and as he went swept the barrel across the group of men.

'Go to Trittel,' said Freytag to Gombert, 'and tell him to bring coffee up to me on the bridge.'

'With two cups,' added Dr Caspary, who suddenly raised his head, smiled and walked over to Rethorn, who was standing with folded arms under the shrouds. They shook hands, talked together and looked at the place where the mine had exploded.

Freytag climbed up onto the bridge, walking without a glance past the members of his crew who had come up on deck when they heard the first shots and had watched the blowing up of the mine. He felt their disapproval and their anticipation, he felt their longing for a sign, for a call to action or merely to be let in on his own plans. In their attitude lay disappointment over every action that had not been taken, and for which they held him responsible. He still felt all this when he was standing on the bridge looking at them. *They won't understand*, he thought. *They won't understand that it is for their sake that nothing must happen. If we start something, they will be the first to pay for it.*

Patches of rain haze drifted across the bay, obscuring the islands, obscuring the horizon. An airplane flew up and passed invisibly over them, and a dull rumble ran across the bay, coming from the artillery range on the coast.

A good sky for cod, thought Freytag. *If they weren't here I should throw out the hand line.*

He went to the companion ladder, saw Trittel coming up with the coffee, which he carried past Freytag into the chartroom and served with stricken servility, afterwards walking out backwards with the tray in his hand.

'Go and lie down,' said Freytag.

The cook turned around, startled, nodded, moved towards the companion ladder and immediately recoiled when he saw Dr Caspary coming up to the bridge wearing an air of forced gaiety.

'I want nothing from you,' said Dr Caspary, 'except a cup of coffee.'

'It's all right, Karl,' said Freytag, and Trittel squeezed past the two men.

They stood facing each other and drinking black coffee, felt the warm steam on their faces and the hot pressure inside them after the first gulp. Again Dr Caspary offered the skipper a cigarette, again Freytag refused, pointing to the cold cigarette that he held pressed flat between his gnarled fingers.

'You still owe me something, Captain,' said Caspary, putting down his cup. 'You still owe me some time as a listener. I don't think I have told you everything about myself yet.'

'There are people about whom one knows quite enough when they say nothing,' said Freytag.

'There are such people – but I'm not one of them,' said Dr Caspary.

'Why do you want to tell it to me?'

'I don't quite know, Captain. But I surmise that it is

because I have met in you a man who is closest to myself. Our closeness does not spring from what we have in common, but from the completeness with which in every respect we contradict one another. You would be dismayed if you knew how well I understand you and how close we are as we face each other. Your life, Captain, would have been the only one I could have led if I had not decided upon my life, or upon my three lives. I have already told you about the first – it consisted in taking over my only brother's legal practice. Well, the second life arose out of the first. In my legal practice I quickly came to see that everyone can be found guilty of a punishable offense if one only looks hard enough. Everyone, absolutely everyone, is capable of being an accused person – rich and poor, widows and orphans. Take any person at random and I guarantee that something can be found in his life which according to the law of the land would cost him two years in jail – without an excessively harsh sentence. That the whole world has not yet become one great court of law is due solely to the fact that judges are overworked and that at present no one is prepared to accuse himself. That was how I discovered a new life: I wanted to find out what the difference was between those who are arrested and put on trial and those who, although accused, run around free. I wanted to discover how much one can do, how many crimes one can commit, without it showing in one's face and without the court becoming interested. So alongside my life as a lawyer I led a life as – well, I can only say as a convict at liberty. Under the style of a well-known entrepreneur I built up the biggest legal enterprise – you will say, blackmail business – West Germany has ever known. I specialized in investigating the life of highly esteemed and apparently honorable people and then sending them the results of my efforts accompanied with a bill. You will be amazed: only one of my bills was ever returned – and that was solely

113

because in the meantime the accused person had died – all the others were paid. I must add that in my private court I exercised the most scrupulous attention to legal detail and I doubt whether any regular court of law can take more care over the preparation of evidence than I did. I don't wish to overlook the fact that we live nowadays in the age of lawyers – in which every minor employer rings up his attorney to inquire about possible legal consequences before sleeping with his secretary.

'Anyhow, my second life brought me success such as I could never have achieved as a lawyer. Finally my third life, which I financed from the proceeds of the second, was that of a modest boatbuilder. Bearing my brother's death in mind, I devoted my boatbuilding yard to the development of various types of unsinkable lifeboats – for passenger steamers, for fishing smacks, for all kinds of shipwrecks. The boat from which you picked us up, incidentally, was one of my own manufacture, an early experimental model.'

'And the other two?' asked Freytag, who had listened up to this point without apparent interest.

'You mean the Kuhl brothers?'

'Yes.'

'I am indebted to them for help with my second life. Our relationship goes far beyond the bounds of friendship.'

'So one can see,' said Freytag. 'You are simply made for one another.'

'Eugen isn't feeling very well today,' said Dr Caspary.

'That may be the fault of the pure air here,' said Freytag.

'Possibly. The air doesn't suit me very well either. You'll be surprised, Captain, but I already feel that I have been on this ship too long.'

'You know, you're not the only one to feel that,' said Freytag. 'Your sentiment is shared by others.'

'Listen,' said Dr Caspary, and he quickly glanced around as if to make sure there was no one on the bridge besides themselves; then he took Freytag by the arm and drew him into the wing of the bridge.

'I should like to say something to you, Captain, frankly, just between ourselves.' He spoke in a different tone, and Freytag imagined that he could now detect fear in his voice. 'I want to make you an offer, Captain, an offer such as you have never received in your life. If you will help me to escape I will pay you for it. Take me to the coast – I shall show you the spot at which you can put me ashore – and I will pay you thirty thousand marks. I have the money here, and if you agree I can pay you at once.'

'Is that all you consider yourself worth?' asked Freytag.

'I can raise the price,' said Dr Caspary. 'How much? You fix the figure.'

'For you alone or for your friends as well?'

'For me *and* my friends.'

'That's what I wanted to know,' said Freytag.

'The ship is on its last watch in any case; it will be towed back to port and never come out here again. A final detour would mean nothing to you, but what it would earn you could assure you a comfortable retirement. What do you think of the offer, Captain?'

'You would like to know, would you?' asked Freytag.

'Name your conditions.'

'I have no conditions to name. I am thinking of the man lying down below in the sailroom, whom you shot. That is your offer. I am sticking to this offer and to no other. I had to accept it because I had no choice, but you may rest assured that you will receive a counteroffer. Forget everything you have said to me and don't try to say it to me again.'

'Shall we never come to an understanding, Captain?'

'You said yourself that we understood one another very well, didn't you? Good, then understand me this

115

time too: I have no thought but to get you off this ship – one way or another; I am thinking of the dead man and of the day when we shall be free on this ship.'

'You could achieve that very quickly,' said Dr Caspary. 'My offer remains open.'

'No one on this ship will accept such an offer.'

'Once before I admired your certainty – I do so again.'

'No one,' reiterated Freytag. 'Nor will this ship leave her position before we are officially recalled. That will be decided by the Coast Guard Office.'

'So you said before, Captain.'

'So much the better, then you can save yourself a disappointment.'

'Listen, Captain, I do not presume to give you advice, but on one point – though I don't know why – I should like to warn you: I should like to warn you against the arrogance of being so sure of other people.'

'Captain wanted in the wireless cabin!' shouted a voice, and Freytag stood still for a moment, as though wondering whether to answer the call; then, while Philippi's voice shouted again 'Captain wanted in the wireless cabin,' he turned around and said:

'I don't wish to hide anything from you; you should know what I think of you and what my aims are: you will lose, however strong you may feel.'

Philippi was waiting for him, and as Freytag entered the wireless cabin he slammed the roller door behind him, bolted it from inside, whipped around, his hands pressed flat against the door. On his hawk's face lay a hint of satisfaction. His thumbs rubbed rhythmically over the door, producing a sound that was hollow and distinct, like a casual roll of drums.

'Well?' asked Freytag. 'What has happened? What do you want me for?'

'When this week is up I'm getting out,' said Philippi.

'We're all getting out, everyone on board knows that.'

'We shall never be on a steamer again.'

'Did you call me here to tell me that?' asked Freytag.

'No,' said Philippi, 'that was only my introduction. I wanted to tell you that the Coast Guard Office has been informed. They know what's going on on board.'

Freytag looked at him distrustfully, reached for his handkerchief with his fingers and twisted it around his hand so that the stuff was stretched over his knuckles.

'They know all about it,' said Philippi.

'Who told them?'

'I sent out a message,' said Philippi. 'The Coast Guard Office has been informed who is on board and what has happened. They had to know.'

'So,' said Freytag softly, 'they had to know. You decided that.'

'I considered it my duty.'

'So, you considered it your duty.'

'The Coast Guard Office has a right to know everything.'

'And what will the Coast Guard Office do – now that they know everything?'

'At any rate something, and more than you've done. They will send a boat.'

'You see? That's just what I thought. The Coast Guard Office will send a boat. And what then?'

'Now something will happen,' said Philippi. 'That's what I had to tell you.'

'You're like the others,' said Freytag. 'You all think something absolutely must happen. You're determined to take some kind of immediate action. It's like a disease.'

Freytag eyed him without bitterness, with tranquil resignation, as though looking through him at some ultimate ground. It was not he who was surprised, but Philippi, surprised that the reaction which he had expected and for which he was prepared did not take place. The expression of stubborn satisfaction on his face gave way to an uncertain astonishment, and he pushed himself away from the door, went to his table, on which a box of hand-rolled cigarettes stood, took one, lit it. He had imagined that he was taking Freytag unawares, and now he felt taken unawares himself by the captain's lack of surprise.

'When are they sending the boat?' asked Freytag.

'I don't know,' said Philippi.

'Is it already on the way?'

'They didn't say.'

'Then we shall wait,' said Freytag, 'wait and prepare for trouble.'

'What do you mean?'

'Everything I say.'

First they sent Soltow, and the mechanic came into the chartroom while Freytag was writing up the log, waited, shifted about impatiently behind the chair and finally said:

'They're all fore by the capstan. They're waiting for you.'

'Good,' said Freytag, and he went on writing, he wrote out the pages which he had written before and which Dr Caspary had torn out, he continued the log as far as this hazy evening, and when he had finished Soltow came in again.

'It's time you came,' he said. 'They're all anxious to see you.'

'Who?' asked Freytag.

'All of us,' said Soltow. 'We're all fore by the anchor capstan waiting for you.'

'What is supposed to happen there?'

'You'll see, come with me.'

Freytag put the log away in the chart table, locked the door, and put the key in his pocket. He knew it was the evening on which the time limit that Dr Caspary had set him was up – a hazy evening, murky, washed-out. The sea was empty, the ship was swinging around in the current, a light wind that seemed to be wearied by the gray desolation of the waters made the black ball on the signal line swing lethargically to and fro, and the islands opposite grew flatter and flatter as though sinking into a valley of twilight. Freytag hadn't imagined anything would happen – on the contrary, he had expected Dr Caspary to repeat his offer, raising the price – and in the security of this supposition he had gone to the chartroom and written up the logbook, taking it as far as the evening on which the time limit was up. Pleased with this, he looked at Soltow and asked:

'Who sent you?'

'He personally,' said Soltow. 'Next time he intended to come and look for you himself.'

'I'm coming,' said Freytag.

'There are only two of them,' whispered Soltow. 'One is missing. I was surprised that he didn't come out of the mess any more.'

'A lot of people are going to get a surprise now,' said Freytag.

He let Soltow walk ahead, and thought: *You won't be able to make contact with them. He who won't act as they do is alone. They want to do something at any price, because they're afraid to discover that they might stand alone. Their actions bind them together. There is probably nothing that binds people together so strongly as a common action – if it's something out of the ordinary – and they're sick with it.*

In silence they went down the companion ladder, across the deserted deck, and Freytag stopped and studied the sea once more with his naked eye, fearing that the boat which the Coast Guard Office was going to send them might already be on its way.

The boat was not in sight, the long bay was empty; a

patch of oil was drifting out to sea, smoothing the water, carrying brown grass and pieces of plank and branches along with it.

'Come on,' said Soltow. 'We've been waiting long enough.'

Freytag followed him to the bows, where they were all standing around the capstan, and now that they heard him coming their faces lifted and looked at him – calmly, implacably, without regret. No one took his eyes off him. He was caught in the crossfire of their stares like an airplane at night in the tentacles of the searchlights, and their faces turned with him as he came forward, walked between them and slowly back again. He stood still, looked at them each in turn, his crew and the two others and finally Fred, who was standing alone behind Gombert. Suddenly he went up to Gombert and said:

'Why aren't you on lookout?'

Gombert turned his eyes away, looked without speaking – as though this was the only way he could explain – at Eddie, who was standing with Dr Caspary by the rail; then he shrugged his shoulders.

'Why aren't you all at your posts, where you're supposed to be?' asked Freytag, and as they simply stood there eying him in silence: 'Why aren't you at your post, Philippi? And you, Rethorn?' The cold cigarette wagged about between his lips. He went up to Gombert. He said: 'Go back to the lookout at once, or have you forgotten what you're supposed to be doing?'

'The man will stay here,' said Dr Caspary from the rail.

'He feels very comfortable here,' said Eddie, bringing the submachine gun firmly to his hip.

'Go to your posts,' said Freytag threateningly.

The men looked at Eddie and at Dr Caspary and stayed where they were – obeying an instinctive feeling that seemed to guarantee them safety so long as they remained together. They felt that the first man to leave the group would run the greatest risk; so they stayed and immediately turned again upon Freytag, as though he were directly responsible for what was now happening. They pushed everything onto him and left it to him to remove the compulsion under which they jointly stood. Their faces betrayed this. And on none of the faces did Freytag find a trace of readiness to follow him once more or to entrust themselves to him once more in the expectation that he would act in concert with them; indeed he actually imagined he could see that the compulsion under which they stood was welcome to them, because it made it easier for them to refuse to do what at this moment he demanded of them. He saw this and he turned around to Dr Caspary and said:

'What do you intend to do? Why do you force the crew to stay here in the bows? We have work to do.'

'A man like you doesn't come from another planet,' said Dr Caspary in a soft, mellifluous voice. 'You know what's going on. You've had time to respond to the situation and prevent what we now find ourselves compelled to do.'

Freytag looked around in a flash at his crew and shouted: 'Go to your places!'

They didn't move. Not one of the men obeyed his order.

'Give it up, Captain,' said Dr Caspary. 'Don't try to bring about a situation for which you can't accept responsibility. That's not like you.'

'What do you intend to do?' asked Freytag, although he could see what was going to happen.

'We shall haul in the anchor, and you will put us ashore; it doesn't matter where, just somewhere on land. It won't take long – but at least your ship will be free from its chain for a night.'

'The ship will stay here,' said Freytag, and to the

mechanic: 'Go to your cabin and put the lights on; it's time.'

Soltow didn't move.

'You see?' said Dr Caspary. 'Now your men understand me better than you do. You must see that you stand alone. I'm warning you, Captain.'

'Just try it,' cried Freytag. 'Come here and try to raise the anchor. Come on, which of you is going to be the first to try?' He went to the capstan, placed himself with his back to the drumhead over which the big-linked anchor chain ran, crouched and raised his fists, ready to defend the drumhead against all comers. 'Well, why don't you come?' he said.

'Nothing is sadder than a man who makes himself ridiculous,' said Dr Caspary. 'You're making yourself ridiculous, Captain. Come away from the capstan.'

'The ship will not leave its position.'

'Come away from the capstan,' repeated Dr Caspary softly.

'Come,' said Rethorn suddenly. 'Be sensible and come away from there.'

Freytag looked at him with surprise and suspicion. He took the cold cigarette out of his mouth, rubbed it to pieces between his fingers and involuntarily stepped away from the capstan.

'I thought you had lost your tongue,' said Freytag, 'and all at once you actually start making suggestions to me.'

'They're not my suggestions,' said Rethorn. 'I'm only saying what you've been telling us all the time.'

'Ah,' said Freytag, 'so you're quite prepared to raise the anchor.'

'One man is enough,' said Rethorn.

'Then you're actually willing to help them? Perhaps he made you an offer too?'

'Think of what happened to Zumpe,' said Rethorn.

'I am thinking of it.'

'Then you know enough.'

'Yes,' said Freytag, 'I do know enough, unlike you I know when a thing is worth while. I am quite clear as to what is worth doing and when. That is the difference between us.'

'Get started,' said Dr Caspary, and Eddie echoed: 'Go on, get started!'

No one moved. They stood facing one another as though in an uneven duel and seemed to hesitate only because Freytag was between them. The mute conflict intersected in him, and so long as he stood there, like a magnet drawing their attention to himself like iron filings, nothing happened; but something was bound to happen – and neither he nor the others doubted that – as soon as he moved away. And again Rethorn began:

'Come away from there, or have you forgotten what you preached to us yourself? This is the last watch, in a few days we shall put into port.'

'What of it?'

'It's not worth while.'

'I suppose he has bought you,' said Freytag. 'You speak as if you already had his money in your pocket.'

'Remember what you said to us: no one shall be missing from the ship when we put into port.'

'Things have changed,' said Freytag. 'Sometimes one has to change one's mind, and this moment has now come. The ship will remain at anchor.'

'I'm keeping to what you preached to us before,' said Rethorn.

'Get started, you monuments,' said Eddie, taking a step forward and putting his finger on the trigger. He bared his teeth, leaned his torso slightly back, set his legs apart. The barrel of the submachine gun roamed over the men, then came to a stop pointing at Freytag, and apart from Rethorn the others involuntarily came forward, as though to take the skipper into the security of their group. Fred too involuntarily moved forward with the gliding, uniform movements with which cats withdraw from a danger zone. Pale and erect, with a harassed look in his eyes, he stood behind and to one side of his father, one hand in his pocket, the hand that held the metal marlinspike.

'Don't expect me to start counting,' said Dr Caspary.

'Why not?' said Freytag. 'Counting calms the nerves, and perhaps the anchor will come up of its own accord if you count.'

'For the last time,' said Eddie, 'get started!'

Rethorn went to the capstan, put both hands on the lever and looked at the rusty shackle with which the chain was secured and which had to be undone before the chain could be hauled in, and before Freytag had reached him Eddie sprang between them and raised the submachine gun to cover Rethorn as he went to work.

'Undo the shackle,' ordered Rethorn. 'We're going to haul in the chain.'

No one bent down to unscrew the shackle.

'Take your hands off the capstan,' said Freytag.

'Be sensible,' said Rethorn. 'You know what will happen.'

'I'm coming,' said Freytag.

'Come on then,' said Eddie. 'Just try it.' He lowered the barrel, aimed it firmly at the level of Freytag's belt and put his crooked finger on the trigger. The capstan engine started up with a clatter, working in hissing bursts, but even now no one bent down to undo the shackle.

Freytag's body crumpled up slightly as he took the first step and then, as though it had been set free from a blockage, it advanced with mechanical, ponderous steps towards Eddie, behind whom, perfectly covered, Rethorn stood and now switched off the engine, which ran to a stop with a hoarse grinding noise. And like logs drifting downstream joined together by a chain, the others swayed around them and followed Freytag in the same mechanical and ponderous manner, perhaps not so much voluntarily as under an involuntary compulsion that simply made them ape what he did, so that Eddie, when he saw them all coming towards him, looked back for a second in perplexity at Dr Caspary, like a swimmer who in sudden suspicion turns his head and looks back at the shore. Dr Caspary smiled and nodded to him.

'Look out,' cried Rethorn.

Freytag went on, seeking the eyes of the man who was pointing the gun barrel towards him, he found the eyes, drew them to him, and he saw in them complete alertness and preparedness.

'No further,' said Eddie unexpectedly, and in a low voice: 'No further.'

The others hesitated, stood still, only Freytag moved on towards him, tenaciously now, with short, laborious steps, as though he already felt the resistance emitted by the bluish barrel of the submachine gun, a resistance that was as tangible as a stick whose tip was pressed against his solar plexus. He definitely imagined that he could feel a physical resistance – now that he had heard the truth; and when Eddie fired – a single shot that sounded no different from two boards being banged together: high-pitched, dry and almost disappointing – he supposed for a second merely that the tip of this stick, which he had imagined he felt as a physical resistance, had now been thrust into him. He whipped both hands up and pressed them to his midriff, his face was contorted, his body doubled up, and then he turned around without a sound, fell to his knees and supported himself on his hands, and before his arms gave way and collapsed, Fred had taken the marlinspike out of his pocket. He was no longer looking at his father, he drew the marlinspike out with a movement of the wrist and had to take only half a

125

step to reach Eddie, who had lowered the barrel of the gun and was still aiming it at Freytag.

Fred did not stab the marlinspike into Eddie's back with all his strength, yet he was shocked and surprised at how deep the thorn-sharp tool pierced his back; the boy was so shocked that he let go of the marlinspike and jumped back and saw Eddie sway – as he had seen people in films sway after being struck by an arrow, while the feathered shaft projected from their backs – and before Philippi had time to snatch the submachine gun from his hand Eddie fell and buried the weapon under his body.

'The other!' shouted Soltow, but Gombert was already beside Dr Caspary. He seized his wrist and twisted his arm around behind him, so that Dr Caspary groaned.

'Now it's your turn,' said Gombert.

'I can see that,' said Dr Caspary. 'You needn't make me feel it.'

'Now you're going to get it all back.'

While he pushed Dr Caspary into the messroom and Soltow and Philippi lifted Eddie up to carry him into the messroom too, Fred and the cook knelt down beside Freytag. Trittel undid his apron and slipped it under the captain's head. Above the belt Fred saw the patch of blood spreading in the fabric of the shirt, and he couldn't help thinking of ink being soaked up by blotting paper.

'Captain,' cried Trittel, 'Captain.'

Except for Philippi, the others came back out of the mess and formed a circle around Freytag; Rethorn too emerged from behind the capstan, and they all stood there until Gombert said: 'I'll take him to his cabin.'

He lifted Freytag and carried him from the bows without putting him down. When they were in the port gangway Soltow cried out: 'A boat! It's heading straight towards us.'

'It can take him ashore right away,' said Rethorn.

'Keep quiet, you,' said Gombert. 'Don't ever open your mouth here again!'

He put Freytag down carefully, Trittel pushed his apron under his head, and Fred knelt alone by his father and looked down at the taut-skinned face that was tense as if with the effort of making a mute protest. One of Freytag's hands twitched, he tried to raise it, to press it to his abdomen, where fire was coursing through his entrails; he couldn't manage it.

'Fred?' he asked suddenly, and then: 'Are we sailing, Fred?'

'No, Father,' said the boy.

'Everything all right?'

'Everything,' said the boy.